Under Far Eastern Skies

Stefania Hartley

The Sicilian Mama

First published by The People's Friend magazine as "Under Eastern Skies"

ISBN-13: 978-1-914606-41-0

Edited by Sandy Salisbury
Cover by Joseph Witchall

Contents

Chapter 1

Singapore, 1930s

"Oh, Shona, don't be such a killjoy," her sister begged, fixing a stiff kiss curl on her cheek. "There will be RAF pilots, navy officers, planters…"

Shona put her Agatha Christie book down on the rattan table. "Lizbeth, we're sailing back to England in a few days." She had stopped calling England "home".

Lizbeth turned away from the cheval mirror and frowned at her with kohl-rimmed eyes. "It doesn't mean that we can't enjoy a little fun while we're still here."

"Of course we can, but you won't have time to become acquainted with someone well enough for a long-distance relationship. Only to leave a little piece of your heart behind."

Her sister pouted and pointed the curling iron

at her. "I am not spending my last days in Singapore reading books in my room—and neither should you!" she declared.

Shona bristled. Wasn't it enough to be bossed around by her parents that her younger sister should do it too?

"Please, Shona. If you don't come, Maman won't let me go!" Lizbeth let her arms flop by her sides like a sad dolly.

At twenty-two, Lizbeth was little older than a child. Shona could hardly remember what that age was like. All the excitement, energy and hopefulness had left her long ago. All she remembered from that time was the feeling of powerlessness.

Even now, at thirty-one, she didn't have the independence and freedom she had imagined the years would earn her. Her sister, too, she knew, despite all her feisty energy, was as powerless as a goldfish in a bowl. And Shona had the power to take her out of that bowl for one night.

"All right, I'll go. Just for you," she replied, relenting.

"Thank you! I love you!"

Lizbeth leaped to hug her then returned to her curling iron and set her hair in perfect Marcel waves.

When they alighted from their taxi a short time later at the sailing club, the tropical night air was heavy with the scent of frangipani and jasmine. The notes of a gramophone drifted languidly from the veranda, mixed with the chatter of people and the clinking of glasses.

"That's the song from the film 'Oh, Sailor, Behave!'!" Lizbeth cried, bright-eyed and overly excited.

Perhaps it wasn't sailors who were in danger of misbehaving that night.

She tugged at Shona's arm. "Look, Danny is here and he's with a pilot. Let's go and talk to them."

"You can go. I'll find us a table."

Before Shona had finished speaking, Lizbeth had already uncoupled their arms and was off to join the young planter and his friend.

Shona chose a table facing the sea. If the company bored her, as she suspected it would, she could enjoy the view of the South China Sea.

When Lizbeth and the two young men joined her, however, Shona found herself sitting inexplicably on the side facing the bar instead of the sea.

"Boy! Four stengahs here!" Danny called to the waiter.

Half whisky and half water, the stengah was Shona's least favourite drink. Danny hadn't even bothered asking. When the drinks arrived, she didn't want to make trouble for the waiter and accepted her glass.

So here she was, at a party she hadn't wished to attend, sitting on the side of the table she hadn't wanted and sipping a drink she hadn't ordered! Was there any single part of her life where other people didn't do all the choosing for her?

Her father had denied her a formal education because he believed an educated woman intimidated potential suitors. Her mother kept choosing husbands for her despite Shona's protests that she didn't wish to get married.

Why should she wish to go from the yoke of her father's authority to that of another man? Better to remain a spinster. It wasn't by chance that Mary Anning and Jane Austen, both women who had achieved things, had been spinsters.

Every now and then, well-heeled "old maids" or widows stopped over in Singapore during their world tours and joined the local expat social life. Shona listened with enchantment to their stories. They made life without a man look extremely appealing. Of all the women she knew they were the only ones who seemed to be mistresses of their own destiny.

"Shona, Bertie is talking to you." Her sister interrupted her reverie.

What had he said? Was she meant to reply?

"Forgive my sister, she often has her head in the clouds." Lizbeth gave a chuckle, embarrassed. "And I don't mean the kind of head in the cloud you pilots have!"

Bertie smiled smugly. "No, I would say that's not the sort of head in the clouds that women usually have."

Shona frowned. "Excuse me, I totally disagree. Amelia Earhart has just flown solo across the

Atlantic!" she said.

"Earhart isn't a girl, she's a man," Danny ruled with a dismissive flick of his hand.

"Why would you say that?" Shona fired back.

"Well, just look at her!"

"We are in the 1930s, in case you haven't noticed. Do you always strip of feminine status any woman that threatens male supremacy in your field?"

Lizbeth kicked her sister under the table. Bertie didn't even try to hide an eye roll and Danny snorted dismissively before moving the conversation to the upcoming air display.

Shona's stomach roiled as Bertie joined in with tales of his deeds during the last flight display, generously peppered with what were obvious exaggerations.

How could her sister stomach these pompous stuffed shirts who thought so little of women? It must be pure insanity that moved women to relinquish control over their lives into the hands of men such as these.

She couldn't bear Bertie's monologue a moment longer.

"I'm going to visit the powder room," she announced, standing up. The others didn't protest.

Chapter 2

A covered walkway led out of the veranda towards the ladies' powder room. On its right was a little garden of hibiscus, frangipani and cannas. To the left, the beach stretched to the water's edge and boats rested upside down on the sand like enormous turtles. A waxing moon glittered on the calm waters.

Shona knew her sister was too enraptured by Danny to miss her, and the two men were too enraptured by themselves to miss anyone! She folded her frock behind her knees and sat down on the steps that led down to the beach.

Tree frogs and cicadas poured their hearts out in song. Shona opened her lungs to the cooler night air. Moonlight danced on the surface of the water, making the sea sparkle like a sequined dress.

She imagined slipping into one of the sailing boats moored to the jetty and sailing away. Shona loved sailing—the freedom and solitude; the exhilarating power of harnessing the wind in her hands and the boat's obedience to the tiniest movements of the tiller in her grip. A sigh escaped her.

"It's a beautiful night," a deep baritone voice said behind her.

She turned slowly. A man in an evening suit stood behind her. He had deep blue eyes and an aquiline nose. A mane of blond curls gave him a somewhat leonine elegance.

"Yes. I was just admiring the view. What about you?"

He folded his long legs onto the steps and sat down next to her. Suddenly, the stairs felt a lot smaller.

"I could say the same but we both would know that it's not entirely true. Admiring the view wasn't the reason why we've left other people's company, I'm sure."

Shona was surprised. She was used to people saying platitudes they didn't mean and expecting her to do the same back. Such honesty was refreshing and disarming, and he deserved the same.

"You're correct. I was bored with the conversation. Allegedly I'm in the powder room right now. What about you?"

"I left because I was irritated."

"May I ask who or what irritated you?"

"Men who boast about killing a tiger for a trophy. Who shoot an orangutan mother to take her infant as a pet yet still call themselves gentlemen!"

His body thrummed with such passion and energy that the air around him almost shimmered.

Who was he? He didn't seem like any of the men Shona had met. There was something wild and untamed about him, yet gentlemanly all the same. The blond curls that grazed the back of his shirt's collar and the white dinner jacket instead of a uniform suggested that he wasn't in the Forces.

He couldn't be in the civil services, like her father, or she would have met him before. He could be a banker or a trader. Judging by his rugged looks he was most likely a planter—or an adventurer. She was burning to ask him but didn't.

"Killing such magnificent animals as tigers and orangutans is beyond my understanding. Even reptiles get my sympathy. I could never have a crocodile handbag or snakeskin shoes," she confessed.

"Sadly not many people think this way." He rested his elbows on his knees and looked to the horizon. "We keep felling the jungle to make way for more rubber plantations, granite quarries and tin mines but we still have only discovered and catalogued a tiny fraction of the species that live there. Some of the plants that will be extinct could have been medicinal or future crops. It will be too late if we don't stop destroying the jungle at this rate." His deep blue eyes darkened.

"I guess that you're not a planter."

"You guess correctly." He smiled and a dimple

formed on the side of his cheek.

"Nor are you a pilot, soldier or sailor."

He cocked an eyebrow. "What makes you say that?"

"You have a look about you." Wild, unruly and exciting.

He chuckled. "That's a very polite way to tell me that I need a haircut."

"Oh, no, I didn't mean that. Your hair looks… fine." "Fine" didn't even begin to describe what she thought of his curls, nor how she longed to run her fingers through them. "What do you do here in Singapore?"

"I'm here to get supplies before returning to the jungle across the Strait in Malaya. I'm a botanist."

"A botanist!"

She struggled to keep the awe out of her voice. If she had been allowed to enrol in university, botany would have been her chosen subject.

"It's not as glamorous as it might sound. I live in a tin-roofed hut and my only company are monkeys."

She imagined him swinging through the trees like Tarzan in the motion pictures. Warmth rose up her cheeks and she chased the thought away. "I'm sure it's not a comfortable life but you are doing an important job."

"I am. The jungle needs protecting and we won't do that until we start caring about it. We can't care about what we don't know. My job is to find out what's there and tell others. I believe that knowledge is the first step to love."

The last word surprised her. Other than the vicar in his sermons, the men she knew didn't ever talk about love. That word had never come out of her father's lips and none of the men who had proposed to her over the years had mentioned love.

"You're right, I believe," she replied earnestly. "A very dear friend of mine, an amateur botanist, used to tell me the same thing. Unfortunately, she's passed away."

Chapter 3

Sadness swept over Shona as it did every time she thought of Georgina Hayes. Her friend had been exactly the kind of woman Shona wanted to be—a spinster who spent her life travelling, studying and discovering things.

"She left me a scrapbook of botanical drawings of the Amazon rainforest. As that's a tropical jungle too, perhaps you might find the book useful. I couldn't part with it but I could show it to you," she said, immediately regretting it.

She was leaving soon and she had plenty of things to do in these last few days in Singapore. Meeting up with handsome strangers to show them a book wasn't one of them. Besides, the book was already packed deep in her trunk.

"I'd like that very much," he said with a smile that made her chest fizzle and crackle.

It was too late to backtrack; she had to honour her offer.

Inviting him to her home wasn't a good idea. Her mother would immediately hear wedding bells. The sailing club was a much safer choice.

"Shall we meet here tomorrow morning at ten?"

"That would be smashing." A lovely smile brought back his dimple and lingered in the crinkles around his eyes.

"Shona, here you are!" Lizbeth's voice shook Shona back to attention.

She should be pleased that her sister had finally noticed her absence but she would much rather have continued chatting to the botanist than return to her table. She stood up and he did the same.

"It's been a pleasure talking to you," he told her. "I look forward to seeing you tomorrow."

"Until tomorrow."

As she walked back to the veranda with Lizbeth, Shona realised that they didn't know each other's names. Oh, well, if they missed each other tomorrow so be it. She had plenty of other things to worry about. Like how to stop her sister falling for a planter or a pilot whom she would never see again.

When they were about to reach the veranda, her sister leaned into her. "So you've met Will Palmer," she whispered.

His name was Will Palmer, then.

"How do you know him?"

"Everyone does. Every girl, that is. Achingly handsome, clever, unattached… Unfortunately not marriage material. He lives in the jungle with the wild animals, as far from the world of marriage, babies and family Sunday roasts as a tiger might be from a teashop. He's only twenty-five so he is unlikely to retire soon from that sort of life. You'd better look elsewhere, sister. I'm sorry."

"I wasn't—I didn't! You know that I'm not interested in men and marriage," Shona replied curtly.

"Maman and Papa are, on your behalf," Lizbeth pointed out.

Shona rolled her eyes.

After the conversation with Will Palmer, Danny and Bertie's company felt even duller than before. The only good thing, she reflected, was that now, from her seat facing the bar, she could keep an eye on the rest of the party.

She was hoping to catch another glimpse of the intriguing botanist but that night she didn't see him again.

Chapter 4

He had been about to leave the club, fed up with the party once the conversation had fallen on the topic of hunting, and had decided to head home. Then, on his way out, he had met this girl and everything about the evening had changed.

What had struck Will about her, even before she turned her warm brown eyes in his direction, was that she was sitting on some scratchy, sandy steps in an evening frock.

Most of the ladies he knew cared about their clothes as passionately as he cared about his books. Either this young woman was different or she was in distress. In the first case, he was intrigued to know her. In the second, he was bound to offer help.

When she turned to him, her blissful expression told him that she wasn't in distress but was merely enjoying the view, and he was hooked.

She had seemed intrigued by him as much as he was fascinated with her. He had wrongfooted her with his remark about needing a haircut—which was true but still not near the top of his priorities —and was sorry to have flustered her.

He wished they had had more time together or that, at least, he had had the presence of mind to ask her name. Luckily he was going to see her again tomorrow.

The taxi stopped in front of his friend's bungalow far too soon. Will hadn't yet had time to clear his head nor prepare answers to David's inevitable questions about the party.

David and his wife, Catherine, had urged him to attend. They would be sad to hear that he hadn't enjoyed the evening and had even fallen out with the hunters. The fact was that the only part of the evening he had enjoyed he was reluctant to share. David might not make too much of his meeting with the interesting young lady but Catherine needed no encouragement. She was always trying to match him with some eligible maiden.

Will opened the squeaky front door slowly and padded inside. Everyone had gone to bed. Good. He padded up the stairs to "his" bedroom, the guest room that David and Catherine always kept ready for him.

David and he were old friends but treated each other like brothers. Whenever Will missed the warmth of a family, David, Catherine and the children were there to welcome him with open arms. Because of this, every time he needed to pop over to Singapore to get supplies, their bungalow was his pied-à-terre. He kept his city clothes and his books in his room and, when he returned, everything was how he had left it. The whole family called it "Will's room" and he had a feeling nobody was allowed to sleep there other than him.

When he joined the family for breakfast the next morning, David glanced up at him.

"How was the party?"

"A mixed bag. Overall it was not my cup of tea."

"Of course it wasn't. It would have been more like a stengah but, then again, you don't like whisky," David teased.

"What didn't you like about the party?" Catherine asked.

Will had noticed how, with men, you could get away with keeping a conversation superficial. Women often would sniff out your avoidance and dig deeper.

He sunk his spoon into a slice of papaya with a bit more force than was necessary. "I had a spat with some planters who apparently enjoy hunting innocent animals for the sake of their hides."

Catherine rolled her eyes. "Oh, dear, I can picture it. Have some kaya toast."

She offered him a plate of toast spread with the coconut jam he loved.

"Thank you. You know how to cheer me up, Catherine."

"Being able to do that is a feminine skill. You need a female presence in your life, as I've often told you." She smiled. "May I ask what the good part of the party was, given that you described it as a 'mixed bag'?"

He regretted calling it that since he had decided not to mention the meeting with the girl. Now he was in a bind because he hated lies of any kind, including white ones. His mother had used them abundantly and he had vowed to himself always to speak the truth or nothing at all. This time he would choose the latter.

"Nothing significant."

"Who was there?" Catherine attacked the topic from a tangent but he knew where she was aiming.

Luckily David and Catherine's seven-year-old son, Jonah, had had enough of adult conversation. "Will you play cricket with me after breakfast, Uncle Will?"

The title he had for him was one both of respect and affection.

Jonah's interruption would have been a perfect diversion if it wasn't for the fact that Will couldn't play cricket with him because of the woman about whom Catherine was trying to find out.

He shot a glance at the clock. Already nine. It would take him fifteen minutes to reach the sailing club if he took David's motorcar or a taxi, more if he cycled. He had better not linger over breakfast.

"Sorry, young man. I'm busy this morning."

"What are your engagements for today?" Catherine asked, ever the detective.

He stuffed a piece of kaya toast into his mouth

STEFANIA HARTLEY

to gain time.

Catherine smiled knowingly. "Do I guess correctly that this morning's engagement is connected with the pleasant part of last night's party?"

She had cornered him.

"Yes, you are. Last night I met someone who owns a book of botanical drawings of the Amazon jungle. They have offered to show me the book this morning."

Catherine put down her fork and smiled. "It's Shona Wells, isn't it?"

Chapter 5

"I don't know her name," Will replied.

"A pretty little thing with intense, inquisitive eyes?" Catherine asked.

"Yes..."

The description fit even if it didn't begin to cover how charming, interesting and attractive the woman actually was.

"Mousy hair, brown eyes?"

He nodded.

"Shona Wells, without a doubt."

A million questions rushed to his lips but Will couldn't voice them—showing Catherine his interest for this woman would plunge her into matchmaking mode.

Will wasn't for matching. He was married to his work. He couldn't fall in love with a woman because he had already fallen in love with orangutans and tigers, pitcher plants and orchids. He had vowed to devote his life to studying and protecting them. There was no place for a woman in his life.

"How did you guess that it was Shona Wells?" was the only question that felt safe enough to ask.

"I can't imagine anyone else willing to listen to you talk about plants. No matter how handsome you are—and you are very handsome—no woman will bear hearing how many petals orchids have unless they are genuinely interested."

He barely registered the compliment. This was his chance to get out of Catherine more information about the mystery girl.

"Is Miss Wells a science scholar, then?"

Catherine shook her head.

"Not as far as I know. I think she may have liked to be but her parents had other plans for her. They are very keen on seeing her married and as soon as possible. She's already thirty-one. She won't have anyone. I feel sorry for her. I imagine her happier in a science lab, like Marie Curie, than in a man's home playing wife, hostess and mother."

"Maybe it depends on who the husband is?" David winked at him.

Oh no, not his friend too!

Catherine snatched the sugar tongs from her son's hands. "I'm sure you've finished your breakfast."

She turned to the nanny. "Please take the children to the nursery."

The Frenchwoman nodded and escorted Jonah and his older sister out of the room.

Will had no doubt that Jonah's playfulness with the sugar tongs wasn't the reason the children had been sent away but because of the adult conversation that was about to ensue. If only he could leave the room as well!

As soon as the boy was gone, Catherine turned to her husband. "I can picture Will making a breach in Shona's heart. Showing him her scrapbook could be an excuse to see him again."

"It could just as well be a genuine shared interest in botanical matters," David argued.

The two of them started debating the situation as if Will wasn't there.

"This conversation is pointless. I am never getting married," he interjected.

"Why not?" Catherine asked as if they hadn't had this conversation many times before.

Will wondered whether she genuinely forgot or merely hoped that he had changed his mind.

"I'm not husband material. The life I lead, the little I can offer lacks all the comforts a woman would expect. My work is incompatible with a family."

"One day you'll have had enough of life in the wilderness."

"I'll cross that bridge when I come to it."

"It might be too late then, Will. Shona is thirty-one and she won't be waiting for you. You should be considering present opportunities with an eye on the future and make any necessary compromises," she finished.

He shook his head. "All I can offer is friendship."

An image from the night before flashed across

his mind—Shona's lips in the moonlight. At that moment, if he hadn't turned away and pinned his gaze on the horizon, he might have done something stupid, like reaching out and brushing his thumb over them.

"Stay away from her, Will. Don't give the poor girl hopes," David told him seriously.

"Don't scare him off, David. They are perfect for each other," Catherine protested. "Anyway, Shona Wells isn't a 'poor girl' who gets her hopes up about men. She has had the pick of all available suitors and rejected everyone. Getting through to her heart isn't easy."

Catherine turned conspiratorially to Will and wagged a finger. "The ones you need to watch out for are her parents. As soon as you show the littlest interest towards each other, they'll start planning your wedding. I am sure that is the sort of behaviour that would make Shona shy away."

Will was about to protest that he wasn't trying to get Shona to agree to be his bride but David caught his eye and shook his head.

Will considered his friends' marriage. David never openly contradicted his wife but instead went ahead with doing what he wanted. It was as if he didn't trust that he could reason with her so he treated her with benign condescension and subterfuges that adults usually reserved for capricious children.

Will felt he could never fall in love with a woman he couldn't talk to or one he didn't consider his equal.

The maid took away the empty dishes and Catherine offered him more kaya toast.

"No, thank you. I'm sorry but I must go."

He was already too late to cycle to the sailing club. He would have to take a taxi.

"Enjoy your morning." She winked.

His taxi reached the sailing club just as another taxi had pulled up outside the lobby.

The cab door opened and a leg appeared. The petite figure that stepped out of the taxi was dressed in a cheerful green and pink frock. It had a flowery pattern that echoed the *sarong kebaya* of the local Peranakan women. The whole effect was sunny, fresh and joyful. Even before she turned to face him, Will knew that it was her.

He paid his own taxi and closed the door with a soft clunk but, although she was halfway up the steps, she must have heard it because she turned. When she saw him, she smiled. Something shifted inside his chest and failed to go back into place.

The girl was even more beautiful in the daylight than in the moonlight. It was as if all the features he had ever appreciated in other women—the shape of a cheekbone, the curve of a nose, the cut of a pair of eyes—had been put together into one perfect woman.

Chapter 6

Last night Shona hadn't appreciated how tall Will was. Now, standing opposite him at the top of the stairs, she couldn't fail to notice how much of him there was.

"Hello, Miss Wells."

He knows my name. The thought left her a little lightheaded. She had imagined herself immune to men but this one unsettled her in a way she had never known before.

She must guard herself, make sure she didn't fall prey to infatuation. There were no men in her plans for her future.

As soon as her parents gave up on marrying her off and relinquished her dowry, she would start living as an independent spinster, like Georgina had.

Free from her father and mother, from any husband or children, she could travel, explore, study and, who knew, perhaps discover something new.

"Hello, Mr Palmer."

"You look..." He stopped and gestured to the door. "After you."

There mustn't be any gallantry between them, she decided. This was not a date. "The doorway is wide enough for both," she pointed out.

Her observation backfired because he offered her his arm. It would be rude to refuse so she placed her hand in the crook of his elbow and they walked through arm in arm, more like a couple than if she had walked in front of him as he'd offered.

He was wearing a short-sleeved shirt and, when she touched his bare forearm, a rogue tingle of pleasure rose from her fingers.

"Would you like to sit on the veranda or inside?" he asked.

"A table on the veranda, facing the sea, would be delightful," she said.

"Of course." He smiled.

Hadn't they met, last night, while they were both admiring the sea?

A waiter directed them to a secluded table shielded by luxuriant pots of hibiscus plants, no doubt mistaking them for a couple on a romantic date. If the waiter had made such an assumption, how many other people would draw the same conclusion?

"May we have that table instead?" She pointed to a table in the middle of the veranda. No intimacy there.

"Of course, ma'am."

As soon as they were seated, Shona put the book down between them. A physical barrier as much as a signal to Will, to herself and to anyone who might be looking that this was a business meeting. "Here is the book."

"Thank you. I really appreciate you showing it to me."

He touched it as reverently as if it was the relic of a saint. As he turned the pages, Shona couldn't take her eyes off his roughened but well-shaped hands.

"How interesting. Many of these plants, or closely related ones, can also be found in the Malayan jungle," he commented.

"I suppose the climate must be very similar."

Her awkwardness had abated now that they were talking about nature.

"The question is whether it is a case of convergent evolution of two species evolving independently in similar environments, or one species has spread across continents," he stated.

Excitement gave her goosebumps. This was the most engaging topic she had discussed with anyone since Georgina's death. "Given the geographical barriers, I would put my money on convergent evolution," she told him.

Chapter 7

They discussed at length the two possibilities and their drinks were still untouched when the waiter came over with the tiffin menu.

"I haven't had such an interesting conversation since the friend who left me this book passed away," Shona admitted.

"I am sorry."

"About me enjoying our conversation?" she chaffed.

"Not at all." He smiled and the dimples she had glimpsed the night before came out to play. "I'm sorry about your friend passing on, Miss Wells."

"You may call me Shona, if you like."

"Thank you. And I'm Will."

She flicked the pages to the dedication. "Here she is. Georgina Hayes."

"Gosh! I didn't know Miss Hayes had explored the Amazon, too."

"Did you know her?" A frisson of excitement ran up Shona's back.

"Alas, no, but I've heard a lot about her. She contributed a lot to our botanical knowledge. So she was your friend?"

The admiration in his eyes warmed her cheeks.

"I did nothing to deserve her friendship other than be enthralled from a very young age by the tales of her travels with which she regaled my family every time she visited. My parents regarded her as an eccentric but harmless middle-aged lady. For me she was an inspiration and a role model. I would like to live like she did. To travel, explore, discover. Few women achieve as much as she did in her life."

Why was she sharing her most intimate wishes with him? They had only just met and he surely didn't care.

"It's easier to leave a mark in the world for a woman who hasn't got duties at home. If I'm not mistaken, Georgina didn't have a husband or children," he pointed out.

"I don't desire either."

He nodded. "I understand."

"Other people don't."

Her parents, for example, as well as friends, family and acquaintances. Whenever she said she preferred being unattached, they gave her pitying looks as if she were trying to make the best of an unfortunate situation.

"I'm not surprised," he told her gravely. "I get the same treatment."

"What? You are a man. Bachelors are seldom

pitied, but spinsters are. Bachelors are never 'left on the shelf'."

"True, but there are still well-meaning people —usually married women intent on marrying off everyone else—who try to match me despite my lifestyle being entirely unsuitable for a wife and a family."

She laughed.

"What's funny?"

"I just can't imagine…" *A man as handsome as you being in any need of matchmaking.* But there was no way she would say that. She scrambled for something else to say. "I believe that they have a point. One day, once you've made your fortune, you will decide to settle down and take a wife. Because 'it is a truth universally acknowledged, that a single man in possession of a good fortune…'"

"Must be in want of a wife?" he finished, recognising Miss Austen's words. "And how would I make this fortune?"

"Selling exotic plants to well-heeled English collectors and garden owners."

Even before she had finished the sentence she knew she shouldn't have said it. Georgina had told her about unscrupulous plant-hunters who plundered pristine forests to smuggle rare plants back to England for exorbitant amounts of money. If she understood Will correctly, he was as far from those greedy adventurers as a policeman would be from a thief. He studied nature to protect it, not to harm it.

Hurt flashed across his eyes. "I'm a researcher, not a plant hunter. I only take specimens for scientific purposes. I have never given one away for money."

"I am sorry, I shouldn't have said that. Do tell me more about your work."

His expression immediately softened. "I study ecology."

"What is that exactly?"

She had heard about this new field but not in detail.

"I study the relationships between living things with each other, and between them and their environment."

As Will told her about his research, his blue eyes were on fire and even the air around him seemed to dance with energy. He was a man with a passion bigger than himself.

Georgina had been like this before malaria had sucked the life out of her. Still, Shona had never felt this tingling of skin and lightness of chest when Georgina spoke.

They continued studying Georgina's book. When they got to the last page, a half-finished sketch appeared. Shona swallowed.

"Are you alright?" Will asked.

"I hate this page," she explained. "It's like staring at Georgina's life cut short."

The caption below the image read that it was a pitcher plant, but only the leaves were drawn in any detail. The pitcher was a rough sketch which conveyed the general shape, nothing more.

"I have tried to imagine what the pitcher might look like but I can't. It is hard to think of the extraordinary things Georgina might have done if she had lived longer."

"Maybe these things weren't meant for her to do."

"Who would do them, then?"

He looked at her and smiled. "You."

Her heart did a somersault. Carrying on Georgina's work would be her ultimate dream, one so bold that she had never dared voicing it even to herself. How could she, a self-taught amateur naturalist, complete the life's work of Cambridge-educated Georgina Hayes? Will must have meant she could complete the illustration of the pitcher plant.

"Even if I knew what this pitcher looked like, I couldn't draw it."

"I didn't mean the sketch." He smiled again.

Her heart fluttered. She wasn't sure whether it was a reaction to his smile or to his words.

"I can help you with that, though." He stood up, took the book in one hand and her hand in the other. "Come."

"Where are we going?" she asked, trying to ignore the delicious feeling of his hand wrapped around hers.

"To the mangroves over there." He pointed to the patch of green beyond the sailing club's beach.

He placed a banknote under his unfinished glass of gin and tonic and, grabbing a pencil from the bar on the way, led her out of the veranda.

Chapter 8

Will walked at an enthusiastic pace and, as his legs were so much longer than hers, Shona had to take extra steps to keep up. His excitement was contagious and soon she was skipping.

Her senses were focused on the surface of her skin that was pressed against his palm. Shona had no idea why they were going to the mangroves and found she didn't care so long as he kept holding her hand.

At the end of the same wooden walkway where they had met the night before they were confronted with a rocky ledge and a small steep drop. Will let go of her hand, glanced at her shoes and twisted his mouth.

"Not ideal. Do you mind if I...?"

Before she could respond, he had scooped her up in his arms and was scrambling down the rocky ledge, holding her tight against his thick khaki shirt.

His chest felt hard and muscled, and he smelled

of bergamot, grass and sea. Her senses were overwhelmed and she was left reeling. It only lasted a moment, then he put her down. Too soon.

What was happening to her? She couldn't become infatuated with a man! There was no place for a husband in her dreams for the future.

Only last night she had warned her sister that they had enough time now only to leave a piece of their hearts behind in Singapore.

Even if her attachment to Will Palmer stayed within the realm of friendship, she would still be sad, she knew, when it was time to say goodbye and sail home. She ought to stop this doomed acquaintance right now.

Shona thought of saying she was late for an appointment but Will took her hand again and led her on under a canopy of casuarina with pink and white orchids dangling from the branches.

The sweet pine scent of the casuarina enveloped her nostrils, mingling with that of the sea. This place was too beautiful, and the hand that held hers too warm and comforting, for her to want to leave.

On the ground leaf litter gave way to soft mud and suddenly they were in the mangroves. The mangrove trees dug their roots into the muddy soil like fingers into soft chocolate dough. Mudskippers retreated into their holes at their approaching steps, and skittish crabs scuttled sideways with their stalk-mounted eyes trained on the human intruders.

Out on the sea in front of her a blade of sunshine cut through the tropical clouds and shone on the island of Pulau Ubin, sitting on the jade-green waters like a matron on a silk sofa. Shona stopped to enjoy the sight.

"It should be only a little further," he promised.

"What should?"

"*Ophelia modulata*, the pitcher plant of Georgina's drawing."

"You've seen it here?"

"Yes. It's one of those plants I was telling you about that live on both sides of the Pacific."

He glanced at her sandals and, for a moment, she imagined that he would take her in his arms again and carry her over the mud. He looked indecisive.

"We had better take our shoes off."

She slipped her sandals off her feet and hung them to the strap of her bag. The mud had the same texture of cornflour mixed with water. It was soft, cool and pleasant between her toes. As a child she would have squealed with delight at the chance to step barefoot in this soft, yielding mud. Why should she feel disappointed at not being carried?

A little further he stopped.

"Here it is. Just where I remembered."

A pitcher hung from the branch of a mangrove, surrounded by leaves identical to those in Georgina's drawing. The pitcher matched the shape of the sketch perfectly. This was the plant that had stoked her curiosity since Georgina's death. Finally she was seeing the real thing.

"Thank you, Will," she said, her voice breaking with emotion.

He scratched the back of his head and grinned with a shyness Shona had never seen in men as handsome as him.

"Did you just say that you remembered where to find it?" she asked.

"More or less, yes. I wouldn't have taken you all this way through mud otherwise. *Ophelia modulata* isn't a common plant."

This man had remembered where to find a single pitcher plant in the middle of a mangrove forest. Was it some superhuman sense he had acquired through living in the jungle?

"I'm impressed."

"It's a necessity in the jungle," he replied self-effacingly.

He opened the book, propped it against his chest and started drawing.

She suspected it couldn't be comfortable or easy to draw in that position, but he didn't seem to mind. He was probably only sketching. How could he match the intricate detail of Georgina's work using a blunt pencil borrowed from the sailing club's bar?

She wanted to peer at his work but she was too far away and he might not like it. Instead, she admired the real-life pitcher.

She had always imagined it in black and white,

not transparent green with deep red specks. There was something sensual about the nectar-filled pitcher which was a death trap for insects. Wasn't sensuality dangerous to humans too? Let this plant be a warning that she shouldn't be here, alone, with a man who stirred her blood with a smile.

"I must be heading back."

"I've finished," he said, turning the book to her.

And there it was. Not a rough sketch but a perfect likeness of the real pitcher, with all its specks and spots, veins and rims. It was so vivid that, at first, she didn't register that it was only in black and white.

As detailed and perfect as Georgina's leaves, this pitcher could have been drawn by a man sitting comfortably at his desk with a complete set of well-sharpened pencils at his disposal.

"You've done a wonderful job, Will! It looks so real that I'd like to reach out and touch it."

He looked at her intensely. "I feel like that too."

What did he mean? He wanted to reach out and touch his own drawing because it was so life-like? He hadn't struck her as the kind of man who would praise himself.

Then she saw something on the opposite page which made her breath snag in her chest. He hadn't just drawn the pitcher. He had drawn *her*.

Will had captured her features with the accuracy of a mirror but he had gone deeper than her skin, her countenance, light and shadow.

On that page of Georgina's sketchbook he had captured her soul.

When he had said that he, too, felt like reaching out and touching, had he meant her face? Panic stirred in the pit of her stomach. Her attraction for him was safe and manageable only if it wasn't reciprocated.

"We must go back. It's very late."

Chapter 9

What on earth had got into him? Will could have kicked himself.

Drawing her portrait was way too intimate a gesture. No wonder the girl had looked horrified and had retreated like a hermit crab in its shell.

The truth was that Will had a habit of drawing anything he found interesting, and Shona Wells was the most interesting thing that had happened to him in eons.

When he was with her, everything around them was more interesting, more colourful and alive. He had never cherished talking to anyone, male or female, as much as he cherished talking to her.

Now that simple portrait had ruined everything.

At the club she had been circumspect, telling him clearly that marriage wasn't in her plans. Yet Will stupidly had drawn her portrait like a man in love.

A taut silence stretched between them as they

walked back to the club. Shona kept two cautious steps ahead of him and he followed behind, being careful not to catch up. He had scared her off and had nobody to blame but himself.

When they reached the rocky outcrop where he had carried her, she quickly scrambled up the rocks before Will could offer any help. Not that he would attempt scooping her up in his arms this time—physical contact with him was probably the last thing she wanted. She might even fear that taking her to the mangroves had been a ruse to be alone with her and try to get closer.

At the end of the beach the awning of the club's veranda flapped in the wind like a race's chequered flag. As soon as they got there, Shona would say goodbye. After that, Will could only hope that she wouldn't avoid him if they met again at a party.

He wanted to tear her portrait from the book, run back to the mangroves and start their trip from the beginning.

She stopped on the steps where they had met and offered her hand for a handshake. This clearly was going to be a formal goodbye.

"Thank you very much for completing Georgina's drawing," she told him. "I hope that her book has been of some use to your research. Please, accept my best wishes for your work in the future."

Will's heart sank further. She was leaving no opening for the possibility of another encounter. He ignored her proffered hand.

"Being able to see the book has been extremely

useful, thank you. To get the maximum benefit from it, however, I ought to cross-reference it with my botanic library."

He paused to give her time to speculate over what he was about to suggest and whether she would agree to it. Shona dropped both her gaze and her hand.

"Would it be inconvenient if I borrowed it overnight?" he begged.

She bit her lip, considering, and rolled one ankle outwards as if the heel of her foot wanted to run away while the ball wanted to stay. Her fingers curled and uncurled around the book, possibly mirroring whatever struggle was going on inside her. Then she lifted her gaze and held his.

"That will be fine. Sometimes personal convenience must be put aside in the interest of the natural sciences and the common good."

What an exquisitely polite way to tell him that she was only saying yes because she cared about his work, and nothing more.

"Thank you," he said humbly.

The way she handed him the book, holding it from its extremity, made it impossible for their fingers to accidentally brush.

"Where and when should I return it to you?"

"Here will be fine. How about tomorrow at ten o'clock?"

"Perfect."

It wasn't. Will would rather have returned it to her home so that he would know her address.

That way he would have felt a little more tethered to her. Still, he had messed up and he had already pushed his luck by asking for extra time to study the book.

"Until tomorrow," she said, still avoiding his gaze.

"I look forward to it."

Will watched her disappear into a taxi and clutched the book to him as if it was a lifeline.

Chapter 10

When Will got back to his friend's house, David was smoking his pipe on the veranda. He habitually spent the hours after Sunday tiffin napping indoors under a cooling fan. He had probably been waiting for Will's return.

"Hello, old sport. How did it go?" David asked him as soon as he was within earshot.

"Tickety-boo."

"Tell me more. Spill the beans."

"Nothing that would interest you. We discussed plants."

Despite their long friendship, David had never shared Will's passion for the natural world.

David patted the rattan chair next to him. "Please."

Will had no desire to share the events of the morning, especially his terrible faux pas, but he felt a debt to David for all his kindness and hospitality so he sat down. His friend asked a servant to get them both a drink. Clearly, this was going to be a longer chat than Will had hoped for.

"This is what it was all about."

He opened the scrapbook and rested it between the arms of their chairs. David glanced at it, then smiled. "That's what you and Miss Wells can tell yourselves, anyway. Why do you have it?"

"I'm borrowing it overnight and returning it tomorrow."

"Tomorrow, eh?" David chuckled. "Couldn't wait a couple of days to see each other again, could you?"

"It's not what you think," Will replied.

David let out a puff of smoke and looked intently into his eyes. Will curled his fingers in the palms of his hands.

"I suspect she asked me to return it tomorrow because she didn't trust me to take care of it for any longer than that."

"What makes you think so?"

"The book was left to her by a beloved friend when she died. She hasn't even entrusted me with her address so we're going to meet at the club again."

"She just wants to keep you away from her parents—which is understandable."

David flicked gently through the pages. As Will told David about Georgina and explained the significance of each specimen, he began to feel at ease again. He could discuss plants any time, and at any length, but not Shona.

Anyway, there was nothing to say. He and

Shona had an affinity of minds that could have blossomed into a beautiful friendship or even collaboration—she knew more about botany than she gave herself credit for— but he had ruined it all with that sketch and one reckless remark.

"I expect that this wasn't drawn by Georgina," David said when he got to Shona's portrait.

Will hadn't expected his friend to reach that page.

"No."

"At breakfast you said that friendship was all you could offer any woman. Have you changed your mind?"

Will cleared his throat. "No. My work is incompatible with marriage and I wouldn't offer a woman anything other than that, unless it was friendship."

Love affairs that weren't legalized by marriage usually ended up hurting the woman, at least her reputation. He wasn't going to risk it.

David pinned him with his gaze. "If, hypothetically, you were in a position to marry someone, would you choose Shona Wells?"

"Yes."

The question, raw and unexpected, had slammed into him like a punch in the sternum and his answer had been a kneejerk reaction. Good grief, how could he say that with such certainty? He barely knew this girl!

David smiled. "I never thought I would see the day."

"I will never be in a position to marry, so this talk is nonsense," Will said curtly. He sprang to his feet, almost knocking over his gin and tonic. "I'm tired; I'm going to take a rest."

The tropical heat must have got to him. A cool shower would result in a cool head which would stop him saying ridiculous things. Will took the book to his room.

In the bathroom, he scooped some water out of the Shanghai jar and poured it over his hot skin. He imagined it sizzling. He smiled, thinking how far he had come since those first days here in the Far East, when he'd thought that a Shanghai jar was a standing bath rather than a water container for showering. He had arrived in Singapore as barely more than a boy and had matured into a man.

Today, however, at the mangroves, he had behaved like an infatuated boy. What was happening to him? He should be spending his time in Singapore playing rugger with the team, watching the cricket with his best friend and going to the swimming pool with David's family. Not taking young ladies into the mangroves and drawing their likeness or wondering how he was going to secure another meeting, as he was doing right now...

He rubbed his hair hard with a towel and stood under the ceiling fan. A beige cheecha lizard ran across the ceiling, narrowly missing the spinning blades. He was like the gecko, living a topsy-turvy life with all his priorities upside down, dodging the blades of a whirring fan.

The *cheecha* chirped triumphantly on the other side of the fan.

Will shrugged into a clean shirt and walked up to the window. The fronds of the traveller's palm swayed prettily in the breeze and a koel bird sang its soothing, two-note melody.

He gripped the windowsill and took a slow breath. Maybe it was normal to crave Shona's company more than other people's and all the activities he had always enjoyed. After all, she was a new friend while David and Catherine were old ones. It was just the allure of the novelty, nothing more.

Chapter 11

Shona cut through the top of her soft-boiled egg, the way her mother had taught her. It was neat and effective but not as satisfying as cracking the shell with the back of the spoon.

Her youngest sister, Beatrice, daubed a drop of egg yolk off her shirt while their mother was busy cutting dainty morsels of papaya. At the other end of the oval table their father read the morning paper, slowly draining his tea. Lizbeth was layering kaya jam onto her toast with uncharacteristic fastidiousness. She looked pale and pinched. Shona felt remorseful. They shouldn't have stayed at the party so late.

"Girls, this morning I'm going to Mr Tan to collect a frock he's made for me. You should come too," their mother announced. "There is still time for him to make something for you before we leave."

"Yes, please!" Beatrice said.

Shona's youngest sister had all the starry-eyed enthusiasm and excitement of a girl of sixteen.

Their mother smiled with satisfaction. "What about you, Lizbeth?"

"Thank you, Maman, I don't need anything."

Lizbeth never refused a new frock, her sister mused. There had to be something wrong with her.

The corners of their mother's lips turned down in displeasure. "Shona, you will accompany me to Mr Tan, won't you?"

"I'm sorry, Maman, but I've booked a boat at the sailing club."

She was also going to be meeting Will Palmer but there was no need for her mother to know that. It was going to be a quick encounter, just enough time to hand over the book, tell him that she was going back to England and say goodbye.

Then she would sail off alone into the deep, blue sea and forget his deep, blue eyes and the hard muscle of his chest.

Her mother's lips thinned. The company of only one out of three daughters clearly wasn't desirable. "How long will you be gone for?"

"All day. I'm taking a picnic."

Sailing was Shona's balm and solace. The only place where she felt empowered and free, at the helm of her own destiny. On land she was controlled and steered by her family, society and its conventions. Out at sea she was in charge: captain of her ship; mistress of her life.

"Are your trunks packed?"

Her mother was looking for reasons to stop her

going, she knew.

"Yes, Maman."

The older woman tutted. "I cannot understand this mania of yours. Other young ladies' idea of relaxation is embroidering, playing bridge, swimming, having tea with friends. You, instead, like to play sailor as if you were a boy. No wonder…"

She didn't finish her sentence but Shona had heard it enough times. "…we can't find a man for you to marry."

"Let her sail, Claire. She'll meet more men at a sailing club than at a bridge party," her father put in from behind his newspaper.

"On a weekday morning?" His wife sniffed. "I doubt we would approve of such an idle man. Not to mention the fact that she is about to embark on a long sea voyage. She will be sick and tired of admiring the sea."

"Then I shall spend our voyage reading," Shona promised.

Her mother rolled her eyes and turned hopefully to Lizbeth. "Are you sure that you wouldn't like a new frock? We won't find a tailor as skilled as Mr Tan in the whole of London."

Lizbeth didn't look up from her plate and continued toying with her slice of toast. "No, Maman. I'm busy this morning."

Their mother gave up and the conversation moved on. Shona kept observing her sister. Something was troubling her. When breakfast was over, Shona stopped her in the corridor. "Are you all right?"

Lizbeth gave Shona a look of innocent surprise but it didn't look genuine. "I'm very well. Why?"

"Nothing, but if there is anything wrong, you know you can talk to me."

Her sister smiled. This time it was sincere. "I know." She disappeared into her room.

What more could Shona do? Whatever was bothering her sister, she clearly wasn't going to tell Shona. The clock on the console chimed half-past nine. Time to get into her sailing clothes and pack her picnic.

Chapter 12

Her taxi arrived quickly and Shona slipped inside it as if it was a lifeboat. The journey took them out of the European quarters, through patches of secondary jungle and past the locals' traditional wooden houses on stilts, then on to wide roads flanked by palm trees.

She was going to miss Singapore's raw, wild beauty once she was back in her parents' London townhouse, she was certain.

With luck, she wouldn't be staying in London for long. As soon as her parents resigned themselves to the fact that she was destined to be a spinster, she would ask her father for her dowry. That would give her the financial independence she needed to live the next chapter of her life. One where she would be an independent woman who travelled and studied the world's flora like Georgina. Now that she was thirty-one, that day must be just round the corner.

She was late to her appointment so, instead of walking through the bar, she reached the veranda from the garden and spotted Will. "I'm sorry if I've kept you waiting."

He must have been expecting her from the other side because he whipped around, looking startled.

She saw him take in her bare legs. His gaze struggled to rise to her face but flicked back down. His throat worked before he finally looked into her eyes.

"Hello," he croaked.

She hadn't worn these shorts to be noticed— they were just her sailing shorts—but his reaction made her skin tingle with pleasure. She stopped herself. This wasn't meant to happen. Nothing good could come out of an attraction between them. Marriage was out of the question for both.

At first, Shona had imagined that they could be friends but now, after the portrait and this look, she wasn't too sure anymore. Thankfully her departure would put an end to any half-witted attachment developing between them.

"Would you like a stengah, a gin and tonic or your usual lemonade?" he offered.

He remembered what she had ordered yesterday, then.

"Nothing, thank you," she replied. "I'm about to set sail. The wind is good now."

He creased his brow in disappointment. Had he imagined that this was a date, she wondered.

She should never have agreed to meeting again. Should have asked him to courier the book to her bungalow. She had wanted to see him again, though. It had been a very bad idea indeed, and it was high time she nipped this relationship in the bud.

"This is my last chance to sail before I leave Singapore. My family is returning to England in a few days," she told him, delivering what she hoped would be the coup de grâce to their ill-fated acquaintance.

"Already back to England?"

The disappointment on his face turned into disbelief.

"Hardly already. We've been here two years."

"Why would you want to return to dreary, rainy England?" he persisted.

"My father's overseas posting has come to an end."

"You could stay behind," he suggested.

"Of course I couldn't!"

"Why? Don't you like it here?"

"I do, I love the tropics. But I can't stay here without my family. I hope that the book has been useful," she added, needing to bring this painful encounter to a swift close.

"Very much so." He pulled the book from his leather satchel and placed it reverently on the table before her. "Thank you so much." He hesitated, as if he wanted to say something else but hadn't yet decided on the right words to use.

"It has been a pleasure meeting you, Will. I wish you all success with your very important work."

She stood up, clutching the book to her chest like a shield. The message she wanted to convey was that goodbye kisses, even if only on the cheeks, were not welcome.

He stood up too and, again, she was surprised by how tall and broad this man was.

"Goodbye Shona. It's been a genuine pleasure knowing you. If you ever wish to keep in touch, you can write to David Rowan, at the District Office. He's a dear friend of mine and I stay with him and his family whenever I'm in Singapore."

"Thank you, I'll keep it in mind. Goodbye, Will," she stammered.

Before she knew it, he bent down and kissed her on both cheeks. Instantly her legs turned a little wobbly and her hands wanted to cup her cheeks to preserve the imprint of his lips. Instead, she gripped the book tighter and left.

The boat workshop was only behind the main building but it felt a million miles away as she walked towards it. She reminded herself that Will hadn't demanded her correspondence address, nor had he extorted promises that they would write to each other. Also, she had got her book back. She had accomplished everything she had set out to, so why wasn't she happy?

She was used to goodbyes—her father's job had given her years of practice. She had said goodbye to beloved nannies, house staff and friends. In most cases she had known that she would never see these people again. So why was this goodbye so hard?

As soon as she was at a safe distance from the veranda, she stopped to collect herself. The sea in front of her was scattered with junks and sampans. Once she was out on the water, she would feel better.

Chapter 13

"**S**orry, ma'am, all the dinghies are taken today. We have another boat ready for you," one of the club's boys told her, showing her to a boat on the slipway, which was ready to be launched.

It was easily the most beautiful sailing boat the club had ever given out for rentals. It was so polished and so obviously cherished that she wouldn't have been surprised to discover that it belonged to the club manager's personal collection. It had happened before that he had let her use one of his boats when all the rentals were taken.

"Thank you very much. She's beautiful."

The boy nodded and grinned.

Shona raced down to the slipway, then froze. This boat wasn't for one person.

It was impossible for one person to control the jib and the main sail as well as the tiller. It was a beautiful sailing boat for two.

Had the club's boys seen her with Will and

assumed they would be sailing together? The idea both repelled and attracted her. No. The whole point of sailing today was to be alone. Will Palmer was the last person she needed on her boat. She strode back up to the workshop to ask for another boat. Any old tub would do so long as she could sail it on her own.

The rental desk was unmanned, the boat storage area deserted, and the workshop silent. Shona saw the boys sitting under the shade of a mango tree, eating their tiffin and snoozing. She wasn't going to disturb them during their break and be the arrogant white woman who expected to be served at any hour. She returned to the slipway and considered.

Yes, the boat was big, but hadn't the Egyptians built pyramids with levers and pulleys? If she were to loosen the lines and guide the boat off the trailer slowly, she could get it into the water on her own. With a little ingenuity, she would also be able to sail it on her own.

She loosened, pushed and guided, and was halfway through her plan when it became apparent that, even with all the ingenuity in the world, the slipway was too short and the tide too low to launch the boat single-handedly. Now she was stuck with the boat halfway off the trailer, too unstable to be left unattended while she went for help.

She gave the boat a push towards the trailer. A shove. A heave. Nothing. Of course this big girl was much heavier going up than down. Boats were swift and graceful on water but cumbersome on land.

"If you take that side, I'll take this one." Will's voice came from behind Shona.

Had he been watching her try to launch, struggle and fail? Her cheeks warmed.

"You don't have to help. If you could call one of the boys to come over, I'll be fine."

"Are you suggesting I'm not as strong as them?" he asked with an impish smile and took the other side of the boat.

"Certainly not," she said quickly. She hadn't failed to notice his broad shoulders and muscled arms.

"Then I'm happy to assist."

It would be ill-mannered to refuse him. "Thank you. At my count of three, we lift the boat off the trailer and into the water."

They did that, and the boat slipped easily into the sea, like something that belonged there. Shona jumped into the boat and lowered the tiller into the water. "Thank you."

"Where's your crew?" he asked while she finished rigging the boat.

"I haven't any."

"This boat is for two people."

"I know." She found the jib sheet but her arm wasn't quite long enough to reach it from the tiller.

"You can't sail her on your own, Shona. Nobody can."

He was right. She could not control the tiller, the mainsheet and the jib sheet at the same time unless she stood in the middle of the boat with her arms stretched awkwardly.

"I have no choice," she told him, exasperated.

"That's not true," he replied. "We always have choices. You can choose to ask me to sail with you, for instance."

We always have choices. It was an intoxicating idea but was it true? In her everyday life it didn't feel like it. "You must have other things to do and other places to be." *Go away and let me deal with this problem on my own,* was what she meant.

"I do but I have choice, too."

The sunshine had turned his blond curls into spun gold and his eyes sparkled against his tanned skin. Why was this clever, handsome man insisting on spending more time with her when he knew that she was leaving in a few days?

"What good can come out of it?" Her question was not just about the sailing trip.

"I don't know but I do know that nothing bad can come out of it either."

Will was wrong about that. Fragments of someone's heart could be left behind; shards of nostalgia could be embedded in what would otherwise have been happy lives.

Was there any point in worrying about that, though? The damage was already done in her own case. Once she left Singapore, she knew, she would think about Will Palmer and miss him whether she took him sailing with her today or not.

The boat's dazzling white sail flapped in the wind, the sea glittered under the sun and the breeze caressed her skin. It was one of those days when mistakes don't exist and everything ended well.

"Right. Would you like to be my crew?"

He knocked his bare heels together in a military salute. "Aye, Captain!"

He stepped onboard. As soon as they had put out from the shore and it was too late for her to change her mind, he spoke casually. "Tell me what do to. I've never sailed before."

Chapter 14

Earlier, when Shona had bid him farewell in a tone that made it clear that she wasn't expecting to see him again, Will had feared their paths weren't going to cross again. Now here he was in a boat with her!

The sun had fired specks of copper in her hair and, with her eyes trained on the island ahead and an expression of competent concentration, she was even more beautiful than before.

This was a happier version of the Shona he had met on land. Gone was the languid melancholy he had seen in her eyes on the night of the party. Even her voice had a different timbre as she instructed him to pull the jib sheet or release it.

"Where are we going?" he asked eventually.

"Pulau Ubin."

She pointed to the lush island ahead of them, almost straight in the direction of the wind.

It always fascinated him how sailing boats managed to zig-zag their way to any destination despite being unable to sail straight into the wind.

Maybe he could zig-zag his way to a friendship with Shona.

She didn't want marriage and certainly he couldn't offer it, but they could be friends. They shared a passion for the natural world, understood each other and enjoyed each other's company. At least, he enjoyed her company. Maybe too much.

"Have you been to Pulau Ubin before?" she asked.

"No."

"I might be able to show you some interesting orchids I found last time I went there."

"Do you sail a lot?"

"A fair bit," she replied. "When I'm sailing, I'm alone. When I'm alone, I'm in charge. I'm free."

Was this why she had resisted him coming along, because she enjoyed being alone? That meant her prickliness hadn't been personal. His chest felt a little lighter. "You're not alone now, yet you're very much in charge."

She laughed. "Because you don't sail."

"Even if I was a consummate sailor, I believe you would still be in charge. It's your boat and your trip."

She narrowed her eyes. "Do you mind?"

"Not a jot." He stretched his legs across the hull.

"You trust a woman at the helm of a boat, then."

"Yes. I trust you."

"How about an aeroplane? Would you trust a woman pilot to fly you across the Atlantic?"

What a strange conversation. Will was about to

joke that he would trust Amelia Earhart a million times more than some male pilots he knew, but Shona looked as if she was expecting a serious answer, so he replied in kind. "I would trust a fully trained female pilot as much as I would trust a male pilot with equal training."

He imagined himself on an aeroplane with Amelia Earhart but realised he would rather be on this boat with Shona.

The wake of a steamship swelled the sea ahead of them.

"Stand by to tack!" she called.

Tack? What was that?

"Ready about?" she added.

"I'm not clear about what you mean."

She must have mistaken this for "all clear".

"Lee ho!"

She pushed the tiller away from her and the boat swerved suddenly. Before he knew it, the main sail was swinging towards him at speed.

"Duck!" Shona shouted.

Her hand pushed him down milliseconds before the boom could slam into his forehead. Shona had pulled him to the other side of the boat, clear of the sail.

Still gripping his shoulder as if the swinging boom, the strong wind or the choppy sea might snatch him from her at any moment, she looked at him, shaking.

"Why didn't you duck? You could have been knocked unconscious or thrown overboard! I could have lost you!"

Of course, she meant this as in "man overboard", he was sure, but maybe she also cared about him a little bit.

She let go of his shoulder and pulled the mainsheet tighter. The sail stopped quivering but her body didn't and her knuckles remained white around the tiller. "I'm sorry. I overreacted."

"It's no problem and thank you for saving my head from a nasty bump." *And showing me that you care*, he added silently.

Chapter 15

Had she no self-control? She must have lost her mind when she accepted him on the boat instead of calling off the trip.

The next tack went much more smoothly, with Will swapping sides effortlessly with the sail at the right time. He was a quick learner and, a couple of tacks later, they were working perfectly as a team. Strangely, Shona found she didn't miss her solitude, nor was she feeling her freedom encroached upon by his presence.

They reached her favourite bay on the island, where a wooden jetty stuck out into the calm waters.

Will leapt off the boat, secured it to the mooring and offered her his hand to get out of the boat. It was a gentlemanly gesture but she preferred to do it herself. She was the host and he the guest, after all.

"May I carry your bag?" he offered courteously.

"We can take it in turns."

She led the way and he fell into step beside

her. They walked in comfortable silence past beds of cannas, hairy rambutans and smelly durians. Ficus trees sent their long aerial roots to the ground and orchids of all shades of pink, purple and yellow adorned their branches.

A skittish family of mousedeer crossed their path and long-tailed macaques alerted the rest of the island with their excited shrieks of these human visitors. Tree frogs and cicadas provided background percussion.

"I hope you like Marmite sandwiches because that's what I've brought," she told him.

"You don't have to share your picnic. I can find plenty to eat in the forest," he assured her, pointing to a mango tree.

"I'm sure you can but you're my guest. Do you like Marmite?"

"I love it. I haven't had it in ages, though."

"How long have you been away from England?" she asked.

"Four years. I left as soon as I finished my studies, when I was twenty-one."

He was younger than her. She would never have guessed.

"How about you?" he asked.

"We came to Singapore two years ago. I had never been away from England, although I had always dreamed of travelling."

"Look," Will said, slowing down.

A male bird had made a little dancing stage on the ground in front of them and was showing off his brightly coloured feathers to an inconspicuously brown female perched on a branch just above him. Shona and Will stopped and watched the show.

"Just by looking at them you would never guess that these two belong to the same species," Will whispered in awe.

"Yet there are more similarities between these two birds than between male and female humans," she speculated.

"In what way?"

"Both these birds are allowed to fly," she answered wryly.

"Amelia Earhart flies like any man," he countered.

"She's not the average woman. For one thing, she hasn't got a family."

"She is married, though. Marriage doesn't have to be the end of a woman's ambitions."

Shona considered this. "It depends on the man she marries, I suppose."

In an interview, Amelia had described her marriage as a partnership with dual controls. How many men would agree to such an arrangement? Would Will? Not that it mattered to her, of course.

Eventually the female bird flew away and the male stopped dancing. If a bird could show emotions, this poor chap looked forlorn.

"Sorry, birdie," Shona said, smiling.

"Better luck next time, old sport," Will added.

They reached a small beach fringed with palms.

Its white sand glittered like sugar crystals and felt like sugar underfoot, too. This was one of Shona's favourite spots on the island.

She pulled a picnic blanket from her bag and stretched it under a casuarina tree. Sandwiches, water bottle, papaya, knife—she laid it all out on the blanket.

"I'm afraid our picnic is a little sparse. I wasn't prepared for guests."

"I don't need anything except a knife. May I borrow yours?"

"Of course."

She passed him her knife and he dropped it into his pocket. He took off his shoes and belt and, before she knew, he was halfway up a coconut palm, headed for the bunch of lush green fruits at the top. Holding her knife between his teeth, he was using the soles of his feet and his belt to maintain traction up the palm's smooth trunk.

Effortlessly he reached the top and cut the stalks of two coconuts. The fruit dropped onto the sand, rolled down the beach and plopped into the water, where they floated.

In the blink of an eye, Will climbed down the palm and dived into the water. With a few elegant strokes, he recovered the coconuts and returned them to the shore. As he emerged from the waters with his blond locks glistening in the sun, he looked like a sea god. Suddenly there was not enough air to breathe. Shona looked away and busied herself with the sandwiches.

He joined her on the picnic blanket, stabbed the top of one of the coconuts with the knife and levered a chunk off to make an opening for drinking.

"Yours," he said, offering her the fruit.

"Thank you." She gulped down the deliciously sweet water.

He opened the other coconut, drank, then wiped his mouth with the back of his hand. He must have had sand on his hand because now there was sand on his cheek, she saw.

She wanted to reach out and wipe it away but that wouldn't be appropriate. Neither was staring at his face, which she knew she was doing.

She averted her gaze only to meet his eyes, and something shifted between them. They looked at each other for the longest time. Will's eyes were deep and dark. An overwhelming urge to kiss him pulled her towards him like gravity. Her eyelids fluttered, she leaned closer...

Suddenly he got up. "We should go for a little walk."

She reeled back. "Y-yes."

What had got into her? She had been about to kiss him!

She must apologize. Or maybe not. Acknowledging that almost-kiss would give it substance and reality. Better to pretend it had never happened and forget about it all the sooner.

This was probably just what Will was doing. Up on his feet, leg muscles twitching like a racehorse's, he was already putting his shoes back on.

"We must pack up the picnic. I wouldn't trust the macaques with it," he commented lightly, busying himself with the remains of their picnic.

Chapter 16

The sandwiches were still untouched and Shona packed them into her bag.

If Will hadn't stopped it, she would have kissed him! She couldn't trust herself to be alone with him anymore. They should go to the quarries where there would be other people so they wouldn't be alone. She had spotted nice orchids there during previous visits.

"Have you ever been to the granite quarries?"

"No. I'd be very happy to see them," he told her. Was there relief in his voice?

They headed in that direction. It was easier to find distraction once they were in the jungle—from the tree canopy to the undergrowth there was a lot going on.

An orangutan mother and her infant swung between branches; pitcher plants hung like cornucopias of nectar for insects and small animals, and rivulets of leaf-cutting ants snaked up and down tree trunks with freshly harvested leaves on their backs. The racket of hornbills, cicadas and tree frogs made conversation redundant and silence comfortable.

Will stopped to examine some bell-shaped mushrooms. They had such delicate, frilly pink caps that, at first, Shona mistook them for flowers.

"Would you like to record them? You could use Georgina's book. I have it in my bag," she offered.

"That's a good idea."

She handed him the book and a pencil and he flicked over the pages until he got to the one after her portrait. Shona watched him capture every lamella under the mushroom's cap in exquisite detail. This man could be an artist if he wanted to.

Her gaze fell on the label he had written under the picture. *Cookeina Shonensis*.

"It's called Shonensis?" she asked, incredulous. How could it have her name?

"I need to check my reference books, but I don't think it's been discovered yet. If that's the case, I'd like to name it after you—if you have no objection, of course." He looked at her a little sheepishly.

"I'd be very honoured," she stammered.

He beamed. "Let's hope I'm right, then. That's assuming you will let me borrow this scrapbook again so I can compare the drawing with my reference books."

The sentence hung between them. If he borrowed Georgina's book, they would have to meet again, which was the opposite of what she had planned. This sailing trip was meant to be their final goodbye; the only reason she had let him onto her boat was that she wasn't going to see him again. Putting off their goodbye would be prolonging the pain.

"I could bring it back to your home tomorrow," he offered hopefully.

Would it really be such a hardship to grant him his wish? Surely it was safe to see each other again so long as addresses and promises to correspond were not exchanged. The ship headed for England would provide a natural and neat amputation to whatever this was.

"You may borrow it tonight and bring it back to me tomorrow. Shall we say ten o'clock?"

He grinned. "That would be terrific."

Chapter 17

Hurrah, he was going to see her again tomorrow! How he had wanted to kiss her under the casuarina tree! Will was sure that she had wanted to kiss him too. It had taken him every ounce of self-control to get up from the picnic blanket and suggest a walk.

Because what good could come out of a kiss? He shouldn't even be here with her. He should have asked the chaps at the workshop to give her another boat, not offered himself as crew.

A shriek pierced the sky and Shona whipped round.

"What was that?"

"Probably a macaque."

"It sounded like a person."

"Macaques can sound like people."

There was another, more desperate shriek.

"It could be a macaque caught in a trap."

"We must help!"

"It may be hard to find it."

"We can follow the sound."

Had he been on his own, Will wouldn't have hesitated, but how far could Shona walk through thick virgin jungle, the kind through which you had to slash your way with a knife?

"It might be difficult to reach," he warned.

"If there's a trapped animal, we can't leave it to die. I'm going," she declared.

They set off in the direction of the sound using Shona's knife to open a path in the thick vegetation. The shrieks grew more frequent and more desperate until they became hoarse.

Eventually they reached a small clearing where the vegetation had been disturbed. An adult macaque was staring down a hole in the ground, rocking sadly. A feeble voice echoed from somewhere deep below and the adult macaque called back hoarsely.

"I think this mother's infant has fallen into this tin exploration hole."

Tin miners had left exploration boreholes all over the Malayan jungle and, it seemed, on this island. Unmarked, they were quickly covered with vegetation and became booby-traps for people and animals.

Shona took a step forward but he grabbed her wrist.

"Step only where I've already stepped before. There could be other holes."

"Then you'll be the one to fall down!"

"I won't. My head will get stuck," he joked.

Shona didn't look amused.

"Let's grab some sturdy branch before we step anywhere," she replied seriously.

"Okay."

The desperate macaque mother rocked and cried, not leaving the edge of the hole even when they got close.

The shaft was deep, dark and partially hidden by vegetation. The infant's feeble calls echoed from its depth.

"All we can do is lower a rope and hope that the infant has enough sense to hold on to it while we pull it up," he decided.

"What about that liana?" Shona pointed to a mid-sized liana dangling from a tree.

They struggled to disentangle it from the other vegetation but, eventually, managed.

"The infant's voice is getting feebler. What if it's not strong enough to grab onto the liana? Can we lower ourselves into the hole?" Shona asked.

"Not without proper ropes."

Shona nodded.

"Don't worry, baby, we'll get you out of there," she called down the shaft in a sweet soothing voice.

Will's heart melted a little.

They lowered the liana but it hung loose without reaching the infant.

"Let's tie two together," Shona suggested.

"The longer ones are too woody and the suppler ones are too weak. If they snapped mid-way through the rescue, the infant would get hurt."

Will looked around. What could they use that was light, flexible and strong? His belt!

He slipped it from his shorts and tied it to the liana. They tried again but it wasn't long enough.

"Add this." Shona ripped a strip of fabric off her sleeve.

None of the girls he had known would sacrifice a nice shirt for an animal. Will admired her even more.

They tied the strip to the end of the belt to form a cradle, added a small stone to give it weight, then lowered it into the shaft. There was a faint tug at the other end.

"He's in!" Will said.

They pulled the liana up gently. Will's belt emerged, followed by the cradle with the infant macaque snuggled inside it.

The baby blinked in the light and his mother snatched him and leapt up a tree without a backward glance.

"We saved him!" Shona squealed, still showing no regret about the damage she had inflicted to her lovely shirt.

Will slipped his belt back on then gathered some branches to mark the entrance of the hole. The wood would soon be decomposed and new vegetation would cover the hole again but, for a while, he might save some lives by marking it.

"It could have been one of us down that shaft," Shona remarked.

"It's immoral to leave unmarked exploration

holes on the jungle floor."

The thought of her plummeting down a borehole during one of her solo trips to the island tortured Will. Was it normal to feel this way about a woman he had just met?

"We must return to the boat or we won't make it back to the club before sunset."

"I know a quicker way than the one we came. If we follow the quarry road and walk along the coast, we won't have to fight our way through the jungle," she said.

"Lead the way."

They emerged from the jungle and joined a dirt track. In the distance, a hill had been disembowelled for its tin and now looked like a giant had taken a chunk off and discarded it. Will stared at the maimed hill. It stood against the blue sky like a scream of pain. Why did humans need so much while other creatures, small and big, lived on so little?

Chapter 18

"Let's walk on the wet sand; it's quicker," Shona suggested.

She could see the boat moored on the jetty but they were still a little way away and the sun hovered low over the horizon. Tropical sunsets were quick and sailing in the dark without instruments or lights was out of the question.

"I think we've got visitors onboard," Will remarked.

Shona looked up. Oh, no! Macaques were swinging off the boat's mast, tangling the rigging and crumpling the sails. Using their boat as a playground!

Will broke into a run.

"Be off! Shoo!" he roared, waving his arms.

She ran, too, but Will got there first. At the sight of him, the mischievous monkeys abandoned the boat in a flurry of tails and shrieks and dispersed into the forest.

Unfortunately the damage was already done. Every rope was tangled; the sails, horribly crumpled, had come off their guides and lay in a heap, and the emergency oars floated sadly on the water like the flotsam of a shipwreck.

"At least nothing seems to be broken," Will said, assessing the damage.

He must be an optimist by nature, she thought. It was going to take ages to put everything back together and make the boat sailable again. Time they didn't have with the sunset fast approaching.

Sailing in the dark was too dangerous but, on the other hand, if they spent the night together here there would be a scandal. Will would feel bound to marry her, while she would be thought of forever as the old maid who set a trap for a handsome, naïve young bachelor. It was a disastrous predicament for them both.

He must have read her mind because he said, "In the morning, when we sail back, I will jump off the boat a little distance from the shore and swim back the last stretch. No one need know you've been with me tonight."

Was he being considerate, wanting to spare her disgrace, or just worried he'd be pressured into marrying her? She thanked him anyway while marvelling at how sad it was that society and her own family would rather she spent the night alone, exposed to danger, than with a man.

"I'm sorry. You offered to help me and now you're stuck here and are missing your evening engagements."

"I'd much rather be here."

"They must have been unpleasant engagements," she said lightly.

Surely he wouldn't rather be stranded on a wild island without any comforts.

He didn't comment. "While it's light, we should find food, water and shelter for the night," he said instead.

The full magnitude of their predicament dawned on her. Being stranded on the island wasn't just a social disgrace but also a survival challenge! Until they were able to sail home or were rescued, they would need to source water and food, as Will said. The sky was now streaked with pinks and mauves. It would be dark soon.

"I shall gather some fruit for our supper," she said.

As he had already refused to eat her sandwiches earlier out of politeness, Shona felt certain he would refuse them even more firmly now that they were all she had to eat.

"No, I'll go," he argued.

"It's better if you stay here and build us shelters," she explained. "I'm useless at that sort of thing."

Indecision marbled his face. He clearly wasn't happy for her to venture into the jungle at dusk on her own, but he probably agreed that her suggestion made sense. It would soon be dark and ominous clouds towered over the horizon. Shelter was their most urgent need.

"It might rain in the night," she pressed on.

"Very well. I'll stay," he said reluctantly, and she set off.

The jungle was a lot darker than the beach. In the heat of the day the cool shade of the jungle had been a solace but now it was discomforting and menacing. The tree canopies filtered out what little light was left in the sky and Shona struggled to see where she was stepping. She must not step on an unmarked tin-exploration hole or lose her bearings. It was much harder to know her way without the sun for reference. She had better hurry up.

She found a rambutan tree laden with its furry red fruit and a mango tree with its golden wares. Just what she needed.

Did Will like rambutans and mangoes? Living in the jungle for weeks and months at a time, she suspected, he couldn't be a fussy eater. She filled her satchel with rambutans and mangoes. She considered bringing along a big spiky durian too, but it could be more difficult to prepare and she decided against it.

Walking back with her bag full of fruit, she imagined peeling them and laying them out on banana leaves for their supper. It felt a little like homemaking. How strange. The idea of homemaking, of curtains and doilies, sofas and cushions and a man at the head of the table, had always seemed unwelcome. This time it felt different.

Firstly, Will wasn't going to sit imperiously at

the head of the table because there was no table. Secondly, even if Will had sat at the head of the table, he wasn't a traditional man like her father or the men her father had lined up for her through the years.

They would never have accepted to be crew in a boat skippered by a woman, nor let a woman lead the way in the jungle. They'd never have allowed her to go foraging on her own in the dark jungle. Those suitors had made her feel small and helpless. Will didn't. If she had to make a home with a man, she would choose him. He wasn't for the taking, though—he had told her that he would never get married.

The koel bird's plaintive song sounded like the horn of a steamer sailing to England. All her reasonings didn't matter, Shona reminded herself. She was leaving soon.

Chapter 19

Will rested his hands on his hips and looked around him. Sleeping on the boat was out of the question—if those clouds turned into a thunderstorm, the vessel's tall mast would attract lightning.

He must build a shelter on the shore. No, two shelters.

He and Shona had already become dangerously close under the casuarina tree, and it had taken him all his strength to stop himself kissing her. A wise man was one who avoided temptations when he could and who fought against them when he couldn't. Recognizing one's own weaknesses was braver than ignoring them, and the truth was that he had a weakness for this girl as big as the ocean. If he were to let anything happen tonight, he would regret it tomorrow. Worse, she would regret it.

He decided that if he didn't manage to build two shelters before darkness fell, he would sleep outdoors, even if it rained. Meanwhile, he scanned the shore for natural caves or any other good spot. They mustn't be too far from each other, as he wanted to keep guard on Shona, nor from the boat. The pesty monkeys, or other animals, could return and do more damage.

All at once, he spotted a small cave. Perfect! After inspecting the interior to make sure it was uninhabited, he took the rumpled sail out of the boat and draped it over the entrance. The tilt of the ground meant that the cave would remain dry, and the waxed canvas would stop the rain lashing in.

After that, he fashioned a pallet for Shona from some coiled ropes and covered it with the smaller sail like a blanket. It wasn't luxurious, certainly, but she should be able to sleep.

Will certainly wouldn't, but it would be nothing to do with lying outside on the ground and everything to do with the woman who'd be sleeping a few feet away from him. He would be thinking of her all night, he knew.

Where was she? Why wasn't she back yet? Worry crackled through his body like static electricity.

Just then, Shona emerged from the undergrowth and he felt... whole again. By golly, Will hadn't just worried about her, he had missed her. How much more was he going to miss her once she had moved to the other side of the globe? He swatted the thought away.

"I've found some nice treats," she told him proudly.

She arranged the mangoes and rambutans on two large banana leaves as if they were plates.

"Dinner is ready." She smiled.

The words rang of home and domesticity and Will's heart gave a little squeeze. If he could imagine making a home with any woman, here in the jungle, it would be with Shona.

But that could never happen. She had told him that she wasn't interested in marriage, that being tied to a man would be clipping her wings and that she intended to live her life like her friend, Georgina.

What if marriage didn't have to take the same shape for everyone? Could there be a marriage particular to them that didn't clip either of their wings but, instead, let them fly together?

"What are you thinking about?" she asked him.

"Nothing," he replied, suddenly defensive.

"Well, dinner is ready and you're not sitting down to eat. Don't you like any of these?"

He had been so absorbed in his thoughts that he hadn't noticed. "Oh, yes, I certainly do." He sat cross-legged in front of his plate.

"Take what you want," she urged.

I want you. He wanted more meals together, more walks in the jungle, more animal rescues. He wanted this even if the meals were only fruit, the walks were infested with unmarked holes and the rescues meant they wound up with crumpled shirts. Even if they ended up stranded on an uninhabited island with an approaching thunderstorm, Will still wanted to do all these things with her. He wanted to share his life with Shona—hold her in his arms, kiss her, love her. For what could this be if not love?

He would never have any of those things. The most he could have was her company, tonight and tomorrow. Then each of them would go on their own way, oceans dividing them.

Chapter 20

Why was Will so distracted? He seemed melancholy. Perhaps, Shona speculated, he was upset about missing his evening engagements. Dinner parties, dancing at the club, a handsome man like him must have a slew of invitations for every night of the week.

"You're surely being missed tonight," she suggested. "Your friends will be worrying about you. I'm so sorry."

"David and Catherine will be quite unconcerned, I assure you," he replied. "Nobody worries whenever a bachelor stays out overnight."

"Of course," she said stiffly.

The thought of Will in the arms of another woman made her skin crawl. How could she be jealous of a man that she'd only just met, though? She wasn't supposed to get attached to anyone. She had recommended that advice to her sister yet now she had made the very same mistake!

"We had better light a fire before it gets too

dark," he suggested when they'd finished eating. "If your parents have sent a rescue party looking for you, it will help them locate us."

Rescue party. The phrase jarred. The forest glittered with fireflies and resounded with cicadas and tree frogs, the sky was pink and red with the sunset, and Will was with her. How could she need rescuing from all this? She could never say so.

"Good idea," she replied.

He went off to collect firewood and returned with a bundle of twigs and bark. Arranging them neatly on a flat rock, he rubbed together two sticks and eventually a small spark turned into a fire.

"I'll feed it through the night," he told her. This meant that he wasn't intending to sleep.

"We'll take turns," she protested.

"I don't think that's a good idea."

She thought about this. Maybe Will was right. Taking turns would mean waking each other in the night, which felt way too intimate.

She looked at him. The fire was roaring now and the light danced on the perfect angles of his jaw and cheekbones, lighting his hair with a golden coppery glow. Fire could keep you warm, give you light and cook your food, but it could also burn you and kill you.

Will had already lit a spark in her heart and she mustn't allow that spark to turn into a fire lest it hurt her.

She took a sip from her water flask and offered it to him. "Have some water."

"I'm fine, thank you," he said.

"You haven't drunk all day."

"I had the coconut water." He was refusing, she was aware, because he wanted to save the drinking water for her.

"That was a long time ago." She thrust the flask into his hand. "Please. I need you to be well enough tomorrow to help me sail back."

He nodded, took the flask and brought it to his lips, but she could tell that he was only pretending to drink.

A flash of lightning veined the sky, immediately followed by a clap of thunder. A storm was definitely coming. The tower of clouds they had seen earlier hadn't been a false alarm. "We could collect some rainwater in the boat's bailer scoop," she suggested. That way he might finally drink something.

"Good idea. I'm more concerned that the rain will quench our campfire and that we won't be visible to any rescue parties."

She considered this. "I don't believe anybody is going to attempt a rescue during a tropical thunderstorm."

"Hmm, you're right. Then we had better take cover before the rain gets here. You take the cave."

He pointed to a shelter he must have created by blocking off the entrance of a cave with the boat's sail. It looked safe and comfortable. He had done a very good job.

"What about you?" she fretted.

"I'll be over there." He pointed vaguely in the direction of a shallow rocky outcrop which would provide minimal cover. "Don't worry, I'll be able to see your cave from there," he assured her.

Shona wasn't worried about herself. "Those rocks will provide you with no shelter, Will!" Lightning cracked the sky in half. He could be struck! "I won't let you endanger your life out there. If you refuse to take shelter in the cave with me, then I will sit out in the rain with you."

Chapter 21

Mercifully there was enough space in the cave for Shona to sleep on the pallet Will had made for her and for him to sit against the rocks at a proper distance.

"Thank you for making such a comfy bed for me," she told him.

"Not a problem. Goodnight, Shona."

"Goodnight, Will. Sleep tight."

Will nodded. He doubted he would get any sleep at all. He leaned against the wall of the cave, folded his arms on his chest and closed his eyes. If he tried hard enough, maybe he could forget where he was.

Thunder echoed in the sky, then heavy raindrops started pummelling the canvas of the sail. They had made it inside just in time. He hoped that Shona was able to sleep and recuperate.

Time passed, whether minutes or hours he had no idea, then he heard her whisper.

"Are you asleep?"

"Fast asleep," he joked. "Are you uncomfortable?"

"No. I've just got too much on my mind," she said, rustling the canvas as she sat up.

"You must be worrying about your parents."

"Yes, they're one of my worries, but I'm also thinking about London."

"Are you excited, then?"

It hurt to think about her so far away.

"Not at all," she replied. "I won't fit in there anymore."

He considered this. "You won't be staying in London forever, though. You'll be travelling the world, exploring and studying like Georgina."

"Not until my parents give up trying to marry me off and give me my dowry. Until then, I will have to content myself with volunteering at Kew Gardens and the Natural History Museum, attending ladies' lunches and tea parties and being part of London's society."

"You sound as if you don't like the prospect," he remarked.

"I don't. I can't see myself leading that sort of life anymore. I long for the jungle. I yearn to get my fingernails dirty and my skin sunburned."

"Stay here, then." Will tried not to sound too hopeful.

"I can't."

Thunder boomed and lightening lit the cave through the canvas.

"My parents will never allow me to stay back. I have no choice," she continued.

He shook his head. "You know I don't agree with

that. We always have a choice, even if it's only to fight back or to accept a situation. When people try to prevent us having choices, we must take them ourselves."

"It's easy to speak in such a manner for a man with his own means," she countered.

"True, I am a man, but I didn't have any means when I chose to study botany against my parents' wishes and they refused to support me."

"How did you manage?"

"I got a scholarship and also gave private tuition. It was tough. Some days I had to choose between buying books or bread."

"What did you choose?"

"Books, of course." He smiled.

A corner of the canvas lifted and a pair of eyes that looked almost human peeped in.

"I think we have visitors," Will whispered.

In the light coming from the electric sky he made out the silhouette of two macaques, one bigger and one smaller. They tumbled into the cave with a squelch of wet fur.

"Are they the macaques we rescued?" Shona asked.

"I think so."

"Hello, you two," Shona cooed sweetly. "Will, have we any fruit left?"

"I don't think they want food. They're looking for shelter from the rain."

The mother macaque started licking her infant's fur.

"They're so sweet," Shona whispered. "Do you think they'll stay here with us?"

"If they find it comfortable."

Without warning Shona started singing. "Hush, little baby, don't say a word…"

Her voice was as soft as a velvety caress. His mother used to sing that song for him. He joined in. "And if that mockingbird don't sing…"

Their voices blended together in perfect harmony, with his low gravelly notes complementing her high silvery ones.

"Papa's gonna buy you a diamond ring."

A diamond ring. Will imagined going down on one knee and putting an engagement ring on her finger. It was a madcap idea, wasn't it? Until a moment ago he'd have said that he and Shona would never be anything but friends. But hadn't she just told him that she wanted to live in the jungle? She hadn't said "with you" but still…

Wait, she was leaving in a few days. He had no time to let attachments develop and decisions mature in wise, reasoned ways. He would have to act before he lost her to the steamship bound for London.

He had never felt about any woman the way he felt about Shona. The notion of sharing his life with her filled him with joy.

Tomorrow, at the first rays of dawn, he would ask her to marry him. No. Better to wait until they were back at the sailing club. There she would be free, if she wished, to reject him and leave without having to travel back in the boat with him.

The sodden macaques had climbed into Shona's pallet and were listening to her voice, spellbound. Their eyes glinted in the low light and then started closing. Still singing, Shona shifted away from her drenched bedfellows, closer to Will.

Without warning she leaned her head on his shoulder and yielded into his side. She matched him perfectly, as if they had been fashioned to fit together and together was the only way for them to be.

When she reached the end of the song, she tilted her head and looked up at him. Before he knew what he was doing, Will brushed his lips on her forehead in a tender kiss. Her eyes fluttered and closed, and he kissed her on the lips.

The kiss stopped so suddenly that Shona almost ricocheted back.

"I'm sorry, I shouldn't have done that," Will croaked.

Hot shame burst into her cheeks. She had insisted they shared the cave, she had huddled up to him to make space for the macaques, and she had rested her head on his shoulder. By any reckoning it was she who had been too forward.

"I'm the one who's sorry, Will. I didn't mean to— I shouldn't have presumed…"

"No, it's my fault. I shouldn't have come into the cave tonight. I barely managed to stop myself kissing you under the casuarina tree so I should have known better." His voice was raw.

Then she hadn't been mistaken about the almost-kiss under the casuarina tree—he had wanted to kiss her! What had stopped him? "I don't understand."

He took her hands in his. His own were warm, strong and a little rough.

"Shona, you are very special to me. I don't want to do things in the wrong order."

What did he mean by that? Was he going to ask her to marry him? Her chest felt so light that her head spun. Would she say yes?

This morning she had tried to snip off their budding acquaintance. She had told herself that she shouldn't exchange addresses with Will, that ending their acquaintance was necessary if she was to follow Georgina's example. She wanted to walk on her own two legs, without depending on any man. But what if she needed that extra support to walk in Georgina's footsteps?

If she could trust any man to build an equal partnership marriage with her, it had to be Will. He was the only one she could share a home with, here in the jungle. She had fallen in love with him. "Will, I..."

"We should get some sleep now or we'll be too tired tomorrow," he interrupted.

She had been about to confess that she loved

him and that she would be willing to sacrifice some of her independence, but the moment was gone. "Yes."

She snuggled back down into the dry half of her makeshift bed and lay still while her thoughts frolicked.

When was Will going to propose? On this beautiful island or out at sea, with the sea birds and the dolphins as witnesses?

Chapter 22

She must have fallen asleep because, when Shona opened her eyes again, the storm was past. Light filtered through the canvas and the macaques weren't there anymore. Will wasn't there either.

Shona sat up. Had he abandoned her, regretting their kiss and his veiled promises? She lifted the canvas and looked out.

The air was clear and wispy peach-coloured clouds floated above the rising sun like the wind-blown hair of a sky goddess. The sea glittered. But the most beautiful sight was Will walking towards her. Relief flooded her.

He was carrying a pile of pink round balls. "I've got us some breakfast," he announced cheerfully.

"I've never seen this fruit before."

"Because it hasn't been discovered yet by the Europeans. I came across it in the Malayan jungle a few months ago."

"Are you sure it's edible?"

"I've eaten lots and look at me," he said,

grinning.

Shona didn't need to look at him. She had done plenty of that already and had concluded that he was perfect in every way.

"You shouldn't have tried unknown fruit: they could have been poisonous," she warned, feeling protective even if she had no right to be. Yet.

They ate their breakfast quickly and were rigging the boat before the sun was yet clear of the horizon. They had almost finished when the harsh noise of a boat's engine interrupted the slow music of the waves on the shore.

"I think someone has come for you."

A motor launch was heading in their direction. A Navy launch. Had her father sent them for her? Goodness, he hadn't sent it: he was *in* it, looking thunderous.

A seaplane appeared in the cobalt blue sky and, soon after, was landing on the water by the jetty. How many strings had her father pulled to get a boat and a plane? What price would Shona have to pay for it?

The motor launch slowed down as it approached them and she braced herself to face her father.

It wasn't her he was glaring at but Will.

"You won't get away with this!" he snarled.

"Papa, listen, it's not how it looks. Will came because I needed help with the boat. We got stranded here because…"

"Shut up, silly girl."

Her father waved a dismissive hand at her that, for a moment, felt like a slap.

Will stepped between them. "My intentions towards your daughter are honourable, sir. I wish to marry her," he said seriously.

Shona felt as if a cold wave had washed over her. This was Will's proposal?

She had imagined many scenarios but, in all of them, his proposal had been directed to her. "I don't want to do things in the wrong order," he had said. Was this the right order—asking her father before her?

"You wish to marry my daughter?" her father repeated with a hint of incredulity that pricked her pride.

"Yes, sir. I'm asking for her hand in marriage," Will said seriously.

He was asking the wrong person! Shona's gaze bounced between the two men but neither was paying her any attention. Instead, they were staring at each other. How could they not care about her opinion?

Placated, her father spoke to Will as if the two of them were the parties in this prospective marriage. "Come in the boat with me and we'll discuss it on the way."

Shockingly, Will stepped out of her sailing boat and into her father's motor launch without a glance back at her.

Her gut wrenched. Where was the man she had fallen for? This was not the behaviour of a man who would build a marriage as an equal partnership. This was a man who had no regard for a woman's opinion, even on matters that directly concerned her!

Her father had always behaved this way so his words had hurt but not surprised her. Will had made a very different impression on her. But by asking her father for her hand in marriage before asking her, he had disrespected her. She'd never marry him!

Her father turned to her. Was he going to ask her if she wished to marry Will?

No. Instead, he gave her instructions. "You travel back on the seaplane."

Then he turned his back on her and led Will into the cabin.

Stunned, she watched the boat roar off, slicing the water like a knife. Neither her father nor Will gave a fig whether she wanted this marriage or not. They were going to discuss her future without her.

Her father hadn't cared to check whether Will had abducted or blackmailed her. He hadn't even asked her whether she was hurt or in need of medical assistance. All he cared about was restoring the family honour through marriage. To that end he was happy to give her away to a man she might not love. Thank goodness Will Palmer had shown his true colours before trapping her into marriage.

"This way, Miss Wells," a member of the

seaplane's crew said, offering a hand.

"I've a boat to sail back," she said.

"We'll do it, Miss Wells," a sailor told her from the jetty.

She had been so wrapped in her thoughts that she hadn't noticed the two sailors on the jetty, presumably left behind by the motor launch to do just that. Yet another choice that had been taken away from her.

If her boat could be sailed by one person, she might have protested. Instead, she picked up her bag containing Georgina's precious book and climbed into the seaplane.

She looked around at the spartan interior. How very appropriate that, while her father and Will discussed her dowry and price, she was being transported back on a cargo plane.

Chapter 23

Will's plans had actually been quite different. He and Shona would have sailed back together and, on landing at the club's beach, he would have gone down on one knee and taken Shona's hands into his. He would have told her that he had fallen in love with her and would have asked her to marry him.

When her father had called her "silly girl" and looked like he was about to slap her, Will hadn't been able to bear it. He had announced the one thing that was sure to stop this man hurting his daughter or taking her away from him forever.

As soon as he had succeeded in mollifying her father, Will had been so ashamed of bypassing Shona and her wishes altogether that he hadn't been able to look at her. She must be thinking that he was a cad! How was she at this moment? He was desperate to ask for her forgiveness and hold her in his arms, to protect her from any harm.

Right now Shona ought to be in the launch with them. There wasn't anything he would tell her father and not her.

Even if his heart was on the seaplane with Shona, though, he must concentrate on getting into Mr Wells's good books so that he wouldn't stop his daughter marrying him. If she wanted to after this.

The trip in the launch felt like an eternity even though it must have taken a fraction of the time he and Shona had spent on the sailing boat.

Mr Wells asked him detailed questions about his finances and employment. Will answered truthfully even if he didn't give a fig about dowries and money. All he wanted was to marry Shona.

When they finally reached the sailing club, Shona was just disembarking the seaplane. Will leaped onto the jetty and all but ran to her.

As he drew closer, she avoided his gaze and walked away from him.

"Shona!"

She didn't turn.

Will stopped in his tracks. So she didn't want to marry him after all. When she had kissed him back last night, he had assumed that she returned his affection. Maybe he had just been naïve.

He had to hear this from her own lips. He ran after her and stopped in front of her, blocking her way.

"Shona, we need to talk."

Her eyes blazed with anger and he saw she was shaking. "Wouldn't you agree it's a little late?"

"I am sorry. I can explain."

His words sounded lame even to his own ears.

"Nothing to explain. I am never going to marry you. Stay away from me!"

She all but ran away from him towards the clubhouse.

Will felt crushed. How could he have deluded himself into thinking that Shona would want to live in the jungle with him? Or that she reciprocated his affection?

He had no right nor reason to feel hurt by her rejection. Only yesterday morning, when he had returned her book, she had told him a firm goodbye. Later she had resisted his offer to sail with her. Instead, he had wormed his way into spending more time with her.

Now he must respect her will and stay away from her, as she wished. Even if every muscle in his body wanted to run after her. Will sank his feet into the sand and let his ribcage hold the pieces of his heart together while he watched her disappear into her father's car.

Chapter 24

"There was no need for you to run off with the young man and cause a scandal," her father told her sharply as she settled into the car's seat. "I had no reason to disapprove of you marrying him."

Clearly he didn't give a hang if she was hurt or unwell.

"What happened was an accident, not an elopement, Papa," she told him for the second time that morning. "I do not wish to marry him."

She couldn't possibly marry a man who had shut her out of one of the biggest choices in her life. When she had believed she was in love with Will Palmer, she had been mistaken. The man who treated her as equal, respected her choices and valued her decisions didn't exist. He was an illusion.

"We always have choices," Will had said. What he had meant was *he* always had choices. Men had all the power and women were their possessions.

Will was just like her father and all the other

men. Thankfully he had shown his true colours before locking her into a marriage. She had escaped with her life so why were there tears in her eyes?

"I beg your pardon?" her father asked.

"I will never marry Will Palmer."

"You will."

"I cannot marry him."

"What game are you playing, young lady?" he barked.

"You shouldn't be surprised. I was never asked about my intentions."

"You will marry the chap!"

"I cannot obey you in this matter, Papa." Her voice quivered with anger. "I would not be happy with him."

He snorted. "Happiness is a silly romantic notion. What matters is honour. You spent the night together and you should be glad he is willing to marry you. You and that sister of yours must have sawdust in your skulls instead of brains!"

This was too much. If her father insulted her, Shona could bear it, but if he insulted her beloved sister... Her entire body started shaking with rage.

"Lizbeth is more intelligent than anyone else in our family—including you!"

Her father's nostrils flared and he slapped the side of the driver's seat. "Stop the vehicle at once!" he roared.

The driver slammed on the brakes.

"I will not tolerate you talking to your father

like this!" he shouted, too loudly for the confined space of the car.

"Then I shall not talk at all!"

Shona flung the door open, leaped out and slammed the door. The car sped off.

She walked briskly in the opposite direction with her heartbeat in her ears and anger rattling through her body. Eventually she sat down on a milestone, took her water flask out of her satchel and drank the last drops, breathing slowly.

Where was she going to go? She had no money, no food and now no water either.

A cart laden with durian fruits trundled past, the driver looking at her with curiosity. European women didn't sit by the roadside.

Where was she? The inscription on the milestone said that she was seven miles from the General Post Office, the reference point for all the roads on the island. It was a couple of miles' walk back to her parents' bungalow. Enough for her to ponder the foolishness of her outburst and prepare to eat humble pie on her return home. Because home she must go. Until she had financial independence and the means to support herself, she could not rise against her father.

Chapter 25

The walk home was long and exhausting, especially on little sleep and an empty stomach. The fruit Shona had eaten for breakfast had been delicious but not filling, and the heat made her thirsty.

Passersby stared at the white woman in sailing shorts and shirt, bedraggled and alone. No one offered her a lift in their carts and she had no money to pay a taxi or a rickshaw.

When she finally reached the bungalow, sweat was pouring down her brow and temples.

Her father's car wasn't there. Much better this way. She could give her mother her explanation of the story—an accident, not an elopement —without her father contradicting her. If her mother wasn't angry, which was a possibility, she might give her advice on how to placate her father. Shona had never opposed him before so she was in uncharted, turbulent waters.

Shona had barely stepped through the gate when her mother rushed out of the bungalow with an anguished face. Guilt gripped Shona even though her absence had been outside her control.

"Thank God at least one of you is back!" her mother said, grasping her hands.

"What do you mean? Who is missing?"

"Your sister! Didn't you know?"

"No." Shona's heart rate spiked. "Where is Lizbeth?"

Her mother rolled her eyes. "I told your father that I didn't think it was like you both to have orchestrated an elopement together."

"Where is my sister, Maman?" Shona repeated, becoming agitated.

"We don't know."

Dizzy, Shona leaned against the post of the veranda. Her sister was strong in spirit but not in body. If she hadn't left of her own will but been kidnapped... it didn't bear thinking about.

"Your father believed you two were together," her mother explained.

Their father could have looked for Lizbeth elsewhere but he had come to Pulau Ubin because he knew that Shona had sailed there. By not returning home for the night, Shona had delayed her sister's rescue.

"Has Lizbeth left a note? Any clue?"

Her mother shook her head sadly.

If she hadn't left a note then she must have been kidnapped, Shona felt. Still, there might be clues. Had she taken any clothes? What was the last entry in her journal? Shona ran into the bungalow and up to her sister's room.

The bed was unmade but that didn't mean anything. Lizbeth never made her bed. The fact that her petticoat lay limply on the chair next to her bed and her dress was slung over the back of the chair was more worrying. Before leaving the house, especially to elope, Lizbeth would certainly have got dressed and waved her hair.

Shona opened the dresser drawer. Her sister's curling iron wasn't there. Shona smiled to herself. This little detail was enough to tell her for certain that her sister had left of her own accord, taking the essentials. If she could remember every one of her sister's dresses, she would surely find that some were missing from her wardrobe.

Faced with the prospect of leaving Singapore in a few days, Lizbeth had rebelled in the only way she could. She must have eloped with Danny.

He wasn't Shona's favourite by far, but she would have to make herself like the man if she was to share her sister with him.

Maybe it was Bertie? No, Lizbeth had met him for the first time on the night of the party. Her sister wouldn't be as foolish as to run away with someone she barely knew. Unless their imminent return to England had pushed her to desperate measures...

"You were willing to accept a marriage proposal from Will Palmer," a voice whispered inside her. She chased the painful memory away.

Shona opened the drawer of the bureau hoping

her sister hadn't taken her journal with her. Thankfully, the book was still there. The last entry had been written just before the party.

A. will be at the party tonight and we'll discuss the last details for the Big Day. I can't wait.

That wasn't the initial for Danny or Bertie!

First came relief, then the hurt. Her sister had always shared everything with her but hadn't said a word about this man. She had also fooled her into thinking that Danny was the object of her affection. Had that been deliberate or had Shona lost touch with the one person she thought she knew better than herself?

There was no time to dwell on her own feelings now. Their father might be hunting Lizbeth right now. Shona would have to stop him before he got his son-in-law into trouble with the law and alienated the pair forever. She read on.

I have no doubts or reservations about what I am about to do, and the time is right. I will not return to England. I'm going to be a planter's wife.

Shona dropped the journal. Lizbeth had eloped with a planter. Had planned it and put it into action without saying a word to her or dropping the smallest hint.

In Shona's heart hurt for being kept out of her sister's plans was mixed with admiration for her sister's gumption. Lizbeth hadn't waited for permissions, approvals and blessings. Knowing that she wouldn't be allowed to get married before her older sister, realising that Shona wasn't intending to get married, she had taken her life into her hands and had acted upon her wishes.

Her father's car rumbled into the drive. She must tell her parents her discovery and put their minds at rest. Their daughter might have made an unwise choice but she wasn't in danger. As for any other consideration, such as preventing the marriage and avoiding a scandal, it must already be too late.

Chapter 26

Shona ran down the stairs and heard her parents talking.

"The police and forces are on the case."

"I hope they will use discretion. We don't want a scandal." That was her mother.

"Lizbeth hasn't been abducted. She has eloped of her own will," Shona announced from halfway down the stairs.

Her father lifted his gaze. His eyes glinted with anger. "You shouldn't be here. This is no longer your home. You're not my daughter!"

"What?" her mother asked, looking from one to the other with puzzled eyes.

Shona's chest tightened. She hated upsetting her mother. For her sake and that of her sister she would swallow her pride.

"Please, Papa, accept my apology for my behaviour earlier."

"It is not accepted," he said coldly.

"Please, Papa, listen to me! Lizbeth has not been kidnapped. She's eloped. I read it in her journal."

"Nonsense! No daughter of mine would do such a thing."

"What does the journal say? Who has she eloped with?" her mother asked anxiously.

"A planter whose name starts with 'A'. That's all I know."

"Humbug! She would never elope with a planter —they're uncouth drunkards. No, no, she has been abducted. We will find them and punish the culprit. Where is my topee?"

"Where are you going, dear?"

"I intend to join the search with the law-enforcement officers."

"Papa, please!" Shona stood in front of him, blocking his way. "Such a course of action will compromise your relationship with Lizbeth and also with the man who is, possibly, already your son-in-law."

His face grew puce. "The only things that are compromised are Elizabeth's reputation and yours! Out of my sight, strumpet!"

Shona stepped aside and he stormed away. A moment later, he was out of the house with his topee and gun, the latter no doubt loaded.

"I must find Lizbeth before Papa reaches them and arrests her husband, or worse," Shona told her mother. "Do you know any planter whose name starts with 'A'?"

Mrs Wells shook her head. "All the planters I know are already married or too old for Lizbeth." She considered. "Their assistant managers are a lot younger and are all single, but most of them are engaged to girls back home."

"Do any have a name that starts with 'A'?"

"No."

Shona mentally reviewed all her acquaintances. She didn't know any planters personally. Those she had occasionally glimpsed at the clubs—they were recognisable as they wore khaki-coloured shorts and shirts and had sun-weathered skin—seemed too old to be Lizbeth's beau.

Walking into a club and asking a group of strangers whether they knew who Elizabeth's sweetheart might be was out of the question. Besides, women were not allowed in the clubs except for certain occasions.

Her mother turned to her with hopeful eyes. "Have you noticed your sister showing a special attachment towards a young man?"

"I thought I did, but he isn't a planter and his name doesn't start with 'A'."

As she said this, the hurt was renewed.

"You are a poor judge of matters of the heart, Shona. I've often despaired about you," her mother said hurtfully. "Do you know any young planters?"

"No."

She realised she did know someone who spent a lot of time in the jungle, near plantations, and who had spats with planters at parties. Will.

The idea of asking him for help, after the way they had parted, repelled her. Nevertheless, the thought of her sister being attacked by their father like she had been that morning, and possibly being separated from the man she loved, was worse.

Will had mentioned that he was staying with David and Catherine Rowan. She didn't know the couple well but she had been introduced by mutual friends. Shona knew where they lived so finding Will wasn't going to be difficult. Asking him for a favour was another matter, but for her sister she would do anything.

"Maman, I'm going to find Lizbeth and warn her of Papa's intentions."

"You must not! You are already deep in disgrace with your father. He will never forgive you."

She was right, and any other time Shona might have refrained from crossing him further. Not this time. "I am going anyway."

Chapter 27

When Will got back to David and Catherine's bungalow, he found that everyone was out. That was good. He needed time to regroup and prepare answers to the questions his friends were, inevitably, going to ask. He didn't want to tell them fibs but neither did he want to expose Shona to gossip.

He should also pack his trunk so that he could return to the jungle the next morning. The sooner he left Singapore and all the memories of Shona behind him, the better.

There was a knock on the door.

"Come in."

"Sir, there's a young lady looking for you," the housemaid announced.

"A young lady?"

He didn't have lady friends.

"Yes, sir. A beautiful lady," the maid added, giggling behind her hand.

The only beautiful lady he knew was Shona, and there was no way she would be at his door now.

"Where is she?"

"On the veranda."

"Thank you, I'll see her."

He left his room and stopped on the threshold of the veranda. She was wearing different clothes and was sitting on the chair with her back to him but he would recognise Shona even with his eyes closed, he felt.

She was in a pleated skirt and a blouse buttoned-up to her neck, with a large leather bag under her arm and gloves in her hands. Travelling attire. Was she leaving for England already? His heart sank. This was so final. Had she come to say goodbye? That made no sense: she had instructed him, in very clear terms, to stay away from her.

She was smiling at a mynah bird that was perched on the veranda's parapet.

"Hello. May I offer you a drink?" he asked.

She turned and saw him and the smile disappeared. "No, thank you. I have come to ask for your help on a delicate matter."

This must be about last night. Will would do anything to spare her gossip, embarrassment and trouble.

He sat on the wicker chair opposite hers. "You can count on me."

She looked down at her clasped hands in her lap. "Firstly, I must apologise for the way we parted."

"No apology required."

This was the time for Will to explain why he had behaved like a cad when her father stormed in on them. It would require telling her about his feelings for her, however, and this didn't seem like the right time. Having already chosen the wrong time once, he must be a lot more careful now. "How may I help you?"

"This... this is a very delicate matter which requires the utmost discretion."

"That's understood."

"Very well. It concerns my sister Elizabeth." She looked up at him with a hint of anguish in her eyes.

So this wasn't about last night. She had undertaken the mortification of reaching out to him out of love for her sister. Shona must love her very much and Will admired her for that.

She steepled her hands. "Lizbeth has been missing since last night."

"I see."

Had Mr Wells hoped to find both sisters together on Pulau Island and been disappointed and alarmed when he found only Shona?

"Do you know where she might be?" he asked.

"She hasn't left a note and my father is convinced that she's been abducted, but I have read her journal and I have reason to believe that she has eloped. Unfortunately my father is immovable and intends to find her and bring her 'abductor' to justice."

Will could well imagine that.

"He has mobilised the Forces as well as the police force. I fear for my sister and for the man who is, most likely, now her husband. I must find them and warn them before my father reaches them."

"I'll come with you," Will offered without needing to think about it.

"That's not what I came to ask you."

"I'm offering anyway."

He wasn't going to let Shona go alone on this difficult mission. His legs were already twitching to set off.

"The reason I'm here is that Lizbeth mentioned a planter in her journal. His name starts with 'A' and he was at the party. That is all I know. Do you have any idea who he might be?"

Will considered. Anthony McCafferty? It had been he who, at the party, had boasted about orphaning a baby orangutan to make it a pet. Will had been so upset by that conversation he had left the group and had met Shona on the way out. Surely not him! The man was unprincipled and insufferable. How could Shona's sister have fallen in love with him?

Still, Will had worked on near all the plantations of the Malay peninsula and he knew all the plantation managers and their assistants. There was no-one else whose name started with 'A'.

"It must be Anthony McCafferty."

"What do you know about him?" Shona asked, leaning forward.

Expounding his opinion of the man would do no good to anyone. Anthony might make a better husband than Will would give him credit for. Everyone should be given a chance to make a first impression. Shona might already be the man's sister-in-law and Will wasn't going to prejudice her against him. "Not much."

"Do you know his plantation?"

"Yes, I'll take you there."

He had said it without hesitation even if, after their spat at the party, turning up at Anthony's plantation wasn't an attractive prospect. Shona needed his help and he would swallow his pride and do whatever he had to do to help her.

"No need. I can go on my own. I've borrowed a friend's motorcar and I know how to drive."

This was yet another thing he liked about her: she was capable, brave and resolute.

"I'm afraid Anthony's plantation is very remote. The roads to get there are unsuitable for cars. The best way to reach it is by junk or motorboat, up the river Johor."

Her face clouded.

"I'll take you on my boat," he added.

"You have a boat?"

"A motor launch, not a sailing boat. You know that I can't sail."

For a moment, he caught her off guard and almost saw the memories of their sailing trip flit across her face, bringing a brief smile.

She turned serious again. "Why would you do that for me?"

It was a good question but he didn't know the

answer fully.

"Because you must have no one else to help you or you wouldn't have come to me."

"You are helping me out of charity?"

"Charity, chivalry; I'll call it whatever will make you accept it."

Don't call it love. It wasn't love—he had squashed that out of his heart.

"I would be doing a good deed by helping someone else do a good deed, if that makes sense."

"Then I accept, on condition that I'll pay for the fuel and to contact him by wire."

"There's no point sending a wire to Anthony. His plantation is so remote that he would only get it when he goes into town."

In addition, should Anthony have anything to hide, the element of surprise would be in their favour.

Will wrote a note for David and Catherine, asked the cook for some tiffin in a metal carrier, and filled canteens with water. He also packed spare clothes and a rope, just in case, and finally got them a taxi to Changi, where his boat was moored.

Named after his favourite marine flowering plant, the *Posidonia* was his pride and joy. Dutch made, all polished wood and brass, she was faster than anything else on the water.

Will loaded the provisions aboard as well as a spare tank of fuel and a cushion for Shona. Then they set off towards the estuary of the Johor River.

Chapter 28

As they chopped the waters of the Johor River, neither spoke. It wasn't just due to the noise of the engine nor the awkwardness of their situation. Shona's mind was full of worries for her sister.

Was Lizbeth already married to the planter? And was that even to be hoped for?

Will seemed concentrated on his job which didn't look like an easy one. As the estuary turned into the river and they progressed upstream, the mangroves encroached on the navigable space with their tentacle-like aerial roots.

Here a long stem threatened to entangle the propeller; there a floating log turned out to be a crocodile. Everywhere it was difficult to see the course of the river as it branched and meandered.

Traditional, flat-bottomed sampan boats pushed their way upriver with poles like Venetian gondolas. Bumboats carried cargo up and down the river, and the occasional rowing boat made its way through the traffic, too. This bustling thoroughfare was a far cry from the solitary expanse of the sea but Will seemed entirely at ease.

The wind ruffled his hair and made him narrow his eyes. The crinkles around them gave him an even more rugged look. Despite what he had done on Pulau Ubin, he was still an attractive man. *Don't be fooled again, Shona.*

She looked away and stared at the trail of churned foam fanning out behind the engine like the train of a wedding dress. She chased that thought away.

Suddenly the lush, varied and messy forest gave way to a sad expanse of uniform rows. The plantation had started.

"What are they growing here?"

"Pineapples. It gives them revenue while they wait for the rubber trees to mature. Rubber is much sought after for car tyres and electrical wire insulation. But it takes a big initial outlay and a long wait before the trees can be tapped and yield any significant amount."

Eventually they rounded a bend in the river and a black-and-white bungalow appeared at the top of a hill. It had a tiled roof in the colonial fashion, a large veranda and an English-style lawn all around it.

Will steered the boat towards a jetty that barely jutted out of the vegetation. He killed the engine and, as the noise stopped, the humid air was filled by the cacophony of jungle insects, frogs and birds.

Will helped Shona onto the jetty where a large

monitor lizard was sunbathing on the wooden slabs, unconcerned by their presence. They stepped over it and started on the steep path that wound its way up to the bungalow.

"If Anthony turns out not to be our man, what do we say is our reason for this visit?" he asked.

It was a good question. "How well do you know him, Will?"

"Not at all."

"So we cannot trust him to be discreet."

"No."

Will's tone told her that he didn't think highly of the chap.

"Should I hope that Anthony is not the man, perhaps?"

Will averted his gaze. "You'll make up your own mind when you meet him."

And she did so as she looked up and saw in the distance a man in a topee shouting at one of his employees. The man was beefy and tall, with a harsh voice and an angry countenance, while the recipient of his anger was a little old man.

"Please tell me that's not him," she begged Will.

"I'm afraid it is."

Lizbeth could not have fallen in love with this man! This was a hope more than a certainty. Shona couldn't rule out her sister falling for this man— she herself had fallen for someone who had shown no respect for her wishes.

"Hello, Anthony," Will said, interrupting Anthony's tirade.

The planter whipped round. His stance remained aggressive but his expression turned to puzzlement as he took in the visitors.

"Will Palmer," he said in a tone that sounded more challenging than friendly. "What are you doing in these parts? And who is this fair lady?"

"Have you met Miss Shona Wells, sister of Miss Elizabeth Wells?"

If Anthony was her sister's beau, his face would betray recognition. It remained blank. Relief swept through Shona. She didn't want this man as her sister's husband and her brother-in-law.

If Anthony wasn't the man they were looking for, though, who was? Will had said Anthony was the only planter whose name started with "A". Their search for Lizbeth had just started and they'd already hit a wall. Disappointment replaced relief, then panic as she realised they hadn't yet agreed how to justify their visit.

"No, I have never had the pleasure of meeting either lady," Anthony said with an oily smile.

His gaze travelled up and down her in a lecherous way as he walked towards them. He kissed her hand. His lips were hot and sweaty.

"I'm taking Miss Wells on a tour of the plantations of Johor," Will said lightly.

"Then you shall be my guests tonight!"

"I'm afraid we're on a tight schedule and can only stay for a couple of hours," Will told him, to Shona's relief. She had no wish to spend time in this man's company. Besides, they didn't have time to waste.

"Nonsense! You can't tour my plantation in a couple of hours. Anyway, it's not your decision, old sport. We all know that it's the women who rule the roost. Isn't that right, Miss Wells?"

"I'm afraid Mr Palmer is right. We are indeed on a tight schedule."

"Mr Palmer!" he scoffed. "I'm sure you two call each other by first names, or maybe more endearing terms."

Was he hinting they might be lovers?

"We are good friends." Shona stressed the word.

Anthony smiled and she realised that she had played his game. He had wanted to find out the nature of their relationship. Now he knew they were romantically unattached, he might try his luck with her. She cursed herself for her stupidity.

"You must have travelled a fair way and, whatever your destination for the night, it'll be quite a distance. You should stop for a drink," he proposed.

"It's very kind but—"

"Actually, we'd love a drink," Will interrupted.

Shona bristled. Staying with this unpleasant man would delay their search.

It also irked her that Will hadn't consulted her. Not that she should be surprised after what he had done in Pulau Ubin that very morning.

"Excellent, old sport," Anthony said.

He clapped a hand on Will's shoulder so hard that she was sure it must have hurt. She was disliking this man more every moment.

Chapter 29

Anthony led them up to the bungalow where the houseboy, who was sweeping the veranda, disappeared inside with a look of apprehension on his face. Anthony clearly ruled his household by fear.

They sat on the spacious veranda and Anthony mixed a gin sling for Will, soda and lime for her, and a stengah for himself.

She was grateful for the liquid but she couldn't see why Will was giving this man their precious time.

"Tell me about the plantations in this area. Who are your neighbours?" Will asked casually as soon as Anthony joined them on the wicker chairs.

Ah! This was why Will had accepted Anthony's invitation. He wanted to glean information about the other planters so that they could make a guess about where her sister might be. She had misjudged him.

"Hmm, well, on the south there's a Dutchman running a two-thousand-acre timber plantation."

"What's his name again?" Will narrowed his eyes as if he was trying to remember.

"Willem, isn't it? Something like that. Those Dutch are all called Jan or Willem," Anthony replied with a guffaw.

"And your other neighbours?"

"Why the questions? Didn't you do your research before taking a young lady on a plantation tour?"

Will reddened. She couldn't imagine many people having ever accused him of skimping on research. He was knowledgeable, attentive and well-read in any field. If she hadn't sprung this trip on him without warning, he would surely have done plenty of preparation.

"I should have," Will responded humbly.

"Where are you staying tonight?"

"We'll be returning to Singapore," Shona answered quicky.

She could see where this conversation was going and had no desire to spend the night— or indeed a minute more than necessary—as this man's guest.

"That's too far," Anthony protested.

"We were hoping to stop at Charles's plantation," Will told him.

"Charles? That's almost as far a distance as Singapore! I would have imagined that a plant-hunter like you would know his way round the Malay peninsula better than that."

Shona saw Will bristle at the term he used and

squirmed in her chair. Clearly he had bluffed about Charles's plantation. How much more humiliation would he have to endure for her sake?

"If you didn't want to spend the night here, the nearest place is the Dutch fellow but you don't want to go there. The man is a miserable old sod. The second-nearest plantation after that, to our west, is Arthur McGonagall's."

Shona's ears pricked up.

"Don't go there," Anthony repeated. "He's not good company after half-eight in the evening. One of those men who need twelve hours' sleep so, as we all have to get up at five-thirty in the morning for muster, he has to retire with the birds. The fact he's also getting on in years probably doesn't help," he added.

"How old is he?" If Arthur was very old, he couldn't be their man, Shona thought.

"Around forty, I reckon. That's a good old age here in the tropics. In this heat, and with our hard life, we planters become useless by fifty. Then they send us back home where we die a few years later," he finished wryly.

Shona shuddered. Early widowhood didn't sound like a happy outcome for her sister.

"Do planters' wives also die young?" she asked lightly.

"Usually not: they run away before that!" Anthony guffawed. "None of them can take the hardship and solitude of life in the plantation. They go home."

Oh, dear. Why had Lizbeth chosen to marry a planter?

"Why are you asking?" Anthony asked, leaning over her conspiratorially. "Have you got some handsome young planter in your sights?"

The hunting expression repelled and revolted her as much as the smell of alcohol on his breath. "No."

"Does Arthur have a wife?" Will asked.

That was an excellent question. If Arthur was already married, they were no closer to finding Lizbeth.

Anthony guffawed again. "No, no. Never has been and I'd bet my right arm he never will."

Shona smiled. She trusted Anthony's assessment about other people's matters of the heart as much as she trusted a donkey's. The fact that Arthur didn't have a wife could mean that he was still a possibility for Lizbeth.

Would her sister marry a man twenty years her senior? Shona couldn't rule it out. Love was blind. In her own case, it had been enough to stop her seeing that Will wasn't the man she had imagined him to be.

"I would like to visit Arthur's plantation. If he is an early bird, then we should go and visit him at once," she said hopefully, looking at Will.

"Absolutely."

He stood up but Anthony pulled him down on the sofa next to him.

"No, no. You are my guests for tonight. I've

got a new tennis court and no one to play with. We planters lead such a lonely life. You can't take from us such good company." He sent a flirtatious glance to Shona.

"I am no good at tennis."

It was only partly a fib: she wasn't as good as her sister.

"Well, I am sure you can play bridge. All the women in the colony play it from morning till night!" he scoffed.

"I'm the exception," Shona replied.

Anthony frowned. "Then you must accept a tour of my plantation. After all, you told me that you're both here because you are interested in plantations." He narrowed his eyes suspiciously. "Unless there's another reason you two are out on your own." He elbowed Will.

Oh, dear. If spending last night in Pulau Ubin with Will hadn't already ruined her reputation, this man's gossip would. Shona would bet that, next time he was in Singapore, he would be telling everyone at the club about how Will Palmer had taken Miss Shona Wells on an unchaperoned tour.

Did it matter? She was ready to sacrifice her reputation to save her sister's marriage.

"Miss Wells is about to leave Singapore and she wished to visit some plantations before she goes back to Britain," Will said seriously.

"You're leaving Singapore? That's a real shame. Perhaps an eligible young man can persuade you to stay." He looked at her suggestively then stood up.

"Let me show you my kingdom first."

"Okay, let's see it," Will answered.

He had done it again, trampling her right to choose. How could she refuse a tour of the plantation now he had accepted for them both?

Chapter 30

They got up and followed Anthony to the back of the bungalow where a bicycle was leaning against the veranda's railing and a pony was tethered to some stables, across from the house.

"Will, you can take the bicycle," Anthony said, then turned to Shona. "If you don't mind horses, you can ride with me."

I don't mind horses but I mind you, she thought.

In England horse riding had been her favourite activity before sailing had taken its place here in Singapore. Experience told her that this pony couldn't take her weight combined with Anthony's.

"The two of us would be too much for the pony."

He guffawed. "We don't mollycoddle animals here."

Shona had no doubt about that and suspected he didn't mollycoddle people either.

"Anyway, you're not as fat as you think, sweetie," he added, scanning her lecherously again.

She stifled a gasp at his rudeness. "I'll take the other bicycle."

She had spotted another further down the veranda.

"You'll struggle to keep up with us on that."

"Then you'll wait for me," she responded with a false smile.

"How about Miss Wells takes the pony and we gentlemen cycle?" Will suggested, stressing the word "gentlemen".

"Miss Wells can't ride, can she?" Anthony asked hopefully.

"I can. I love riding," she said, enjoying Anthony's disappointment.

With thinly concealed reluctance Anthony handed her the reins of the pony and took the bicycle. They set off.

Shona could tell immediately that the animal wasn't used to being treated gently, and she felt for him.

The rubber plantation was a monotonous expanse of identical rubber trees and the roads, all perpendicular to each other like a giant net, where marked with letters and numbers. Every crossroad looked the same.

"Does anyone ever get lost here?" she asked Anthony when they reached a crossroad.

"Only the natives. They can't read the lot numbers," he replied with contempt.

How she hated this man! She was thankful that

he wasn't her new brother-in-law.

Anthony explained at length the way the trees were tapped for rubber by carving furrows on the bark and letting the sticky sap collect in small earthenware pots tied to the trunks. He kept repeating himself as if Shona might otherwise struggle to follow. She had to bite her tongue a few times and she could sense that Will did too.

She saw that Anthony was sweaty and red with the effort of cycling and guessed he might be agreeable to ending the trip.

"Thank you for this tour. We should head back now."

She hoped fervently they could still make it to Arthur's and avoid spending the night here.

Anthony looked unsure but before he could reply, Will spoke.

"First, would you mind showing us your pineapples?"

Shona had to stop her mouth hanging open with shock. Was Will really so stupid or was he intentionally sabotaging their mission? She couldn't think of a single reason for him to wish to prolong this waste of precious time!

"Yes, they're on the west lot. Let's go," Anthony said with a lot less enthusiasm than he would have had at the beginning of the trip.

Shona darted Will a puzzled glance but he didn't make eye contact. What game was he playing?

Maybe Will Palmer wasn't the honourable man she had believed him to be. Shona had already judged him wrongly, after all. She had taken him for a modern man who believed in equality between sexes and in the right for women's self-determination. It followed she could have easily misjudged him again.

A horrible thought flitted into her mind. Will could be in cahoots with Anthony to harm her reputation, to the point that she would feel that she had to marry him! Well, he was wrong about that. She would never marry him and she certainly would not let him jeopardise her sister's rescue.

She rode along with them towards the west lot, all the while scheming in her mind how she could escape this maze of a plantation and reach Arthur McGonagall's plantation to find her sister.

Chapter 31

Will could see that Shona was furious about this detour. He wished he could confide to her his plan but Anthony was sticking to her like glue.

The cad made his blood boil with all his lecherous flirting with Shona. He would have hated the man's ungentlemanly behaviour if he had used it on any woman, of course, but for Shona to be the target it was one thousand times worse somehow.

"You have no right to be jealous of her," an inner voice whispered. "She's not yours."

He wasn't jealous. He felt sorry for Shona.

They reached the pineapple plantation and Anthony began to tell them about the crop. Will kept an eye on the sun. He had only a vague idea of how to get to the neighbouring plantation from here. Travelling after sunset was dangerous, not only because they could get lost but also because of the tigers and leopards that prowled around.

He could almost feel the daggers Shona was

sending in his direction. He couldn't expect her to guess his plan without knowing the geography of the place, but she would find out soon.

When he could finally see the bungalow of the manager of the neighbouring plantation on top of a hill, he turned to Anthony. "Is that Arthur McGonagall's bungalow?"

"Yes, that's the old man's cave. Look, there is the boundary between our plantations."

"It would make sense if we went straight from here to him, then," Will suggested.

"That's a great idea! It will save us a lot of time," Shona said, jumping at the opportunity.

"You're spending the night with me!" Anthony protested.

"On our way back we will," Will replied.

"But I'll have to ride back on my own," Anthony said plaintively.

"I'm sure that won't be the first time—this is your kingdom, after all," Will joshed.

Anthony had run out of objections but wasn't happy. They said goodbye to him and followed the road out of the plantation.

"I have to confess I was very cross with you when you suggested prolonging our tour to see the pineapples," Shona said as they went along.

"I know you were."

"Now I see it was all part of a plan. But we'll have to return the pony and the bicycle to Anthony. Are we really going to spend the night in his bungalow on our way back?"

He wouldn't care to put Shona under Anthony's lecherous gaze ever again if he could avoid it. It was her choice, though. "Only if you wish to."

"Not in the least!" she said firmly.

"Then we'll sneak back at a time of day when he's out in the fields, leave his pony and bicycle and escape." He paused. "I'm sorry I didn't suggest Arthur as a candidate for our search. His plantation is far from virgin jungle so I've never come across it in my field studies. He never comes to the clubs either, so I don't know him."

"You don't have to explain yourself, Will. What you're doing for me is already above and beyond what I could ever have asked of you."

She mustn't know he wished she would ask much more of him.

"Are you tired of cycling?" she asked solicitously.

"Not at all."

Exercise was just what Will needed to release the anger that Anthony had caused.

"When you suggested to Anthony that he gave me the pony and he rode the bicycle, how did you know that I could ride a horse?"

"I guessed it," he told her, smiling. "You can sail and drive a car so I imagined that, even if you had never ridden a horse before, you would be able to learn on the spot."

The sweet sound of Shona's laughter did strange things to the insides of his chest.

"You have a very high opinion of me. What if I

hadn't been able to learn 'on the spot'?"

Then Will would have insisted on riding the horse himself and would have taken her with him. He wasn't going to say so. "In life one has to take risks."

"Yes," she agreed, turning serious.

All identical in colour and shape, the oil palms of Mr McGonagall's plantation stretched into the horizon like a carpet. A longing for the jungle gripped Will, an emotion as strong as homesickness. He would go back to his work, he vowed, as soon as he had delivered Shona safely to her sister.

Chapter 32

The last rays of the sun were disappearing behind the tops of the palms when they reached the top of the hill where the manager's bungalow sat like a castle. The climb had tired the pony and Shona hoped that Arthur McGonagall had hay and water for him.

McGonagall was on the steps of his veranda waiting for them. He must have seen them from a good distance.

He was a wiry man with grizzled hair, kind blue eyes and a friendly smile. Even if he was on the old side of young, Shona could almost see her sister falling in love with him.

But he was alone. Unless Lizbeth was indoors, they had drawn another blank.

"Good evening. To what do I owe the pleasure of visitors?" The man stepped down from the veranda and came towards them with an outstretched hand.

He seemed genuinely happy to see them, even if they were strangers. Life in a plantation must be very lonely.

How would her party-loving sister cope as a planter's wife?

"Hello. This is Miss Shona Wells and I'm Will Palmer. I'm a botanist," Will said.

Shona's surname didn't bring any flicker of recognition on the man's face. Her sister wasn't here and now it was too late in the day to search for her anywhere else.

Disappointment washed over her and all the weariness of the day and the sleepless night before made themselves felt.

"Arthur McGonagall. Pleased to meet you," the man said with a genuine smile. "Wherever you're heading, it won't be safe to travel in the night. I hope you will be my guests tonight."

"That's very kind and we accept gratefully," Will said after checking with Shona through a quick glance.

"Come inside. My cook has just got dinner ready," Arthur said.

Inside the bungalow the décor was simple but clean. Furniture and shelves were peppered with a mixture of local decorative items, like Royal Selangor pewter goblets, and items from home such as framed photos, well-thumbed novels and a gramophone.

A Malay grammar lay open on a console. Shona had also been learning Malay but, when they had talked to taxi drivers and club staff, she had realised her Malay was nowhere near as good as

Will's.

The table was already laid for three. As soon as they sat down, the cook emerged from the kitchen with a serving dish piled with rice, chicken and vegetables.

Their host smiled at him and the man smiled back, as if they congratulated each other for the perfect timing of the guests' arrival.

"Does Tuan need anything else?" the cook asked.

Beyond the "tuan" address, which meant "sir", it was clear these two were not just boss and employee but also friends.

"No, thank you."

The dish was delicious despite the simple ingredients.

"May I ask to what I owe the pleasure of your visit?" Arthur begged once they had started the meal.

"Miss Wells is about to return to the UK and she expressed the wish to visit some plantations in the area before she goes."

"How nice! If I had received word about it, I would have had a better meal ready and a tour planned for you," Arthur replied without a hint of accusation.

Shona leaned forward. "This meal is delicious and I am so sorry about the lack of notice. I sprang my wish on Will quite abruptly. The steamer to England departs only in a few days' time."

She was trying to stick to the truth as much

as possible. While keeping their mission from Anthony had felt just, deceiving this nice man was somehow wrong.

She wished she could tell him about Lizbeth. Could she? He didn't seem the sort of person who would spread gossip. Besides, if they told him the real reason for their trip, he might be able to help them find her sister. He would know all the planters in the region. The problem was, once the truth was out of the bag, it couldn't be shoved back in.

"That is perfectly understandable. I'm just apologising for the spartan accommodation you'll get tonight here. Apart from my bungalow and that of Reggie, my assistant manager..."—he pointed through the veranda to a faint light on a hill in the distance—"...there's nowhere for you to stay for miles around."

"We are much obliged to you for your hospitality and, again, apologies for the lack of notice," Will replied.

Arthur waved a hand in the air. "No apology is required. I love guests! We live such isolated lives out here that a visit from fellow countryfolks is always a joy. Reggie is fed up of me talking politics, for instance. He's only a young man and I'm sure he wouldn't entertain spending an hour with me if there were more suitable company within a hundred miles! I don't go to town very often so all the news I get is second-hand, through Reggie and the out-of-date newspapers he passes to me."

Arthur sighed. "It's easy to feel forgotten when you live so remotely. Many planters end up drinking too much."

Would this lonely life suit Shona's vibrant sister?

"Don't let me moan and complain. I am really glad that you had the inspiration to visit our plantations out here. The best ideas do come on the spur of the moment," Arthur commented.

Shona put down her fork and spoon and cleared her voice. "Actually there's a specific reason why we are here." She glanced at Will who looked surprised but nodded. "It's a matter that requires the utmost discretion. Can I trust you not to say a word about it?"

"You can," Arthur said seriously.

"My sister, Elizabeth Wells, has been missing since last night. I have reason to believe that she has eloped with a planter whose name starts with 'A'. You will understand why we have just visited Anthony McCafferty's plantation and are here now."

Arthur's face turned grave. "I see. I am sorry to disappoint you. As you might have guessed, your sister hasn't eloped with me." He scratched his chin. "A planter whose first name starts with 'A'... Albert! He's a strapping, good-looking fellow; straight as a die."

This sounded promising.

"Where can we find him?"

"Are you both good riders?"

"Yes," Will replied.

This time it was Shona's turn to be surprised. He hadn't told her that he could ride and, instead, had gallantly let her have the pony all the way.

"Then tomorrow morning, after muster, we'll take three ponies and I'll accompany you to him. He's the next plantation to the north."

This meant it was even further from Singapore. How had her sister got there? She imagined a daredevil escape out of her bedroom window, through the island, over the sea and up the river. With a man Shona hadn't met! It didn't bear thinking about.

Chapter 33

After dinner they played ragtime on the gramophone and talked about the latest political news, the price of rubber and palm oil and the plantation's crop yields.

"The plants are still young so we can't expect more than what we are getting at the moment. Nor can we complain. The prices of commodities are volatile these days and at the last rubber slump many young planters found themselves out of a job, on the streets of Singapore with not a penny to their names."

Shona hadn't known the life of a planter was so precarious. She shivered.

"Why didn't they go back home?"

"Some did but, if there's a rubber slump here, there's likely a recession back home so no jobs for them there either. Many waited it out here in Singapore, living on government handouts and friends' generosity. It pays to be on the spot when the price of rubber rises and companies hire again."

Arthur must have seen Shona's dismay. "Albert isn't into rubber, and his oil palm plantation is doing well. You don't need to worry about your sister's future."

She tried to smile. "I haven't even found her yet."

"Quite. Anyway, we've been lucky here so far," Arthur continued. "We were even able to hire an assistant manager last year. Reggie is a great chap. He's young but he has taken to the job like a duck to water. He works hard, the foremen respect him and everyone likes him. It would be a real loss if the company let him go."

The conversation moved on to other topics and Arthur must have been enjoying their company because time passed but he still didn't retreat to bed.

Will's eyelids were drooping, though. Shona recalled that he, too, had spent the previous night in the cave, probably getting less sleep than her as he didn't have a bed. They should all go to bed and have a good rest.

"If you excuse me, I think I'll turn in," she said, making the first move.

"Me, too," Will said eagerly.

Arthur showed them to the guest rooms then said goodnight and left them to sort out who should sleep where.

Both rooms were spartan in décor and furnishing. One of them, maybe because of the kingfisher picture on the wall or the flowery bedspread, looked more homely.

"Which room do you prefer?" Will asked.

It was a courteous gesture, one she would have expected if, that very morning, he hadn't asked her father for her hand in marriage without consulting her wishes.

That incident was still raw in her mind and she was tired by the long day full of excitement and emotion, so she couldn't help snapping back. "I'm surprised you are interested in my preferences. This morning you were not."

He ricocheted as if she had just slapped him. Truth to tell, she was surprised at her own barb at the end of such a harmonious evening.

"It's unfair to say such things when you haven't given me the chance to explain," he protested.

She leaned against the doorframe. Her feet were aching and her legs, no longer used to riding, were sore. Why had she opened such a can of worms at this time at night? "Fine. Explain."

"I was troubled by the way your father was treating you. I was also afraid that he might prevent us seeing each other again. I told him the one thing that was sure to stop him taking such action."

She straightened up. "You pretended you wanted to marry me in order to placate my father, then."

"I did not!"

"But you did tell him that you wanted to marry me so that he would not whisk me away."

"Yes."

Suddenly she was roiling with anger. How could he have lied about something so important only to mollify her parent? "Do you think that was an honourable way to behave?"

He sighed. "It's not the way I had planned things to go. I was going to make it all right if you had given me the chance."

Did "make it all right" mean taking back his word and explain that it had all been a ruse? "You are a liar and a cad."

He clenched his jaw. "I think you're being unjust."

She felt her cheeks on fire and her eyes sting with tears. "Well, I think you're being a petulant child making flimsy excuses for himself!"

His expression was thunderous. "Is loving a woman a misdeed? Is wishing to marry her a crime? My only mistake was revealing my sincere desire to your father before you. I have just explained why I did that. If you still think that my actions should be punished, to the extent of being called a cad and a liar, then you are a cruel woman, Shona Wells."

She froze. She had got it all wrong. Will loved her. Had wanted her to marry him.

He had asked her father before asking her only because there had been no time. If he didn't tell her father, they would have lost each other.

In return she had rejected him, insulted him and—she recoiled at this the most—hurt him.

Her heart told her to drop on her knees and beg for his forgiveness but every muscle in her body was still stiff with anger, an emotion quicker to come than leave.

"Goodnight, Shona."

Rather than a wish, it sounded like a curse. He strode into the room nearest to him and closed the door.

She didn't try to stop him. Instead, she stood staring at the closed door, unable to summon the courage to knock and beg for forgiveness.

Eventually, she retreated into the other guestroom. And found that the room she had ended up with wasn't the one she had wanted.

Chapter 34

That night, Shona barely slept. It wasn't the croaking of the geckos in her room or the cacophony of the wildlife outside, nor even her worries about her sister.

It was the argument with Will. Once the anger had left her system, the tears had followed—so violent at first that she had to muffle them in her pillow, then soft and self-pitying.

She had called him a cad and a liar, had accused him of things of which he was completely innocent. All this while he was helping her find her sister instead of getting on with his own work. If anyone had behaved like a cad it was her!

He must now think her rude, uncaring and insensitive, and she deserved it.

Mercifully breakfast was a brief affair. She avoided eye contact with Will all through it and he did the same.

Arthur had already been out for muster, despatching the workers to their daily jobs, and had got three ponies ready for them.

Before they set off, as Arthur briefly left them alone at the stable, Shona gathered courage and spoke.

"Will, I'm dreadfully sorry about last night. I had misunderstood you and I unjustly accused you. I don't deserve all that you've done and are doing for me. If you wish to return to Singapore instead of pursuing the search for my sister, I will completely understand."

"I don't turn my back on what I've started. I will help you find your sister, then we will part," he said with a coldness in his voice that cut her more than the anger of the previous night.

It confirmed that he would never forgive her, let alone love her anymore. She must forget what could have been and concentrate on the only thing she had the power to change—her sister's predicament with her father.

As they rode through Arthur's plantation, he commented on problems with the soil or with parasites of the palm, which was alien to Malaya and had been imported from Africa relatively recently.

Will suggested solutions that involved growing it together with other crops that would enrich the soil or protect it from parasites. He also suggested elephant corridors to stop the pachyderms bringing down the boundary fences.

It was hard not to admire Will's intelligence, kindness and knowledge, as well as his elegance and competence as a rider, even if it only made her sadder about her own stupidity.

They crossed the stretch of secondary jungle between Arthur's plantation and Albert's and waded the stream that separated them.

A kingfisher watched them curiously and brought a smile to Shona's lips.

They rode through kampongs made of traditional wooden houses on stilts and reached the road to Albert's bungalow when it was tiffin time.

They rode up to the house without anyone noticing.

"If Albert is not the man we're looking for, shall I tell him that you're touring plantations?" Arthur asked.

"Yes, please."

She was sure it wouldn't be necessary: she felt this bungalow was the place where she'd find her sister. There was an aura of love about it. Anthony's bungalow hadn't felt like a happy place. Arthur's bungalow was a place of friendship and companionship but it was an all-male world. The cook, the houseboy and Arthur. You could sense there were no women there.

This place had a woman's presence. Shona couldn't pinpoint it to anything in particular, certainly not something as obvious as an embroidered curtain or a vase of posies. It was just a feeling that this place was a woman's home and there was love in it. Could her sister have brought about this transformation in just one day?

Arthur stepped onto the veranda and called out Albert's name. A man in his thirties, tall and broad with ruddy cheeks and hair of the colour of fire, rounded the corner.

He was smiling before he saw them and smiled even wider when he saw his neighbour and two visitors.

Shona liked him immediately. He had to be her sister's husband!

But a small dark child was wrapped around one of Albert's legs and he held another one in his arms. Then a Malay woman appeared behind him. There was no doubt that this was a family scene.

"Oh! Hello," Arthur said to the woman with surprise.

"I'm sorry, you haven't met. This is Aisyah."

He didn't say that she was his wife but it was clear that she was the mother of his children, that they were a family and that he was very fond of them.

"Lovely to meet you," Arthur replied, greeting her in the Malay way.

So did Will and Shona.

"Will you stay for tiffin?" Albert asked.

Shona wished she could leave in search of her sister but there were social rules to follow. Also, it would have been unfair to deprive Will and Arthur.

Lunch was a pleasant affair. Will deftly enquired about the names of nearby planters but nobody fitted the bill.

Arthur assured Albert that he had shown Shona around the plantation on the way and that they must be heading home.

Before they set off, Albert took Shona aside. "Thank you for being kind and accepting of Aisyah. A lot of European women frown upon families like mine."

"There's nothing to frown upon. You have a lovely family," she said from the bottom of her heart.

Soon they were back on the road they had come from.

"I'm sorry about that," Arthur told her. "I had no idea Albert had a family. He's kept it very quiet. I believe we wouldn't have found out if we hadn't caught him by surprise."

"It's not your fault, Arthur. It's the fault of a society that makes people like Albert feel the need to hide," Will said seriously.

"I agree," Shona said. "Where could my sister be? Are there any other planters whose names start with 'A'?"

She was despondent. Maybe she should give up, go home and wait there for Lizbeth to make contact or be found by people with more resources and manpower.

"None I know of. Perhaps the best course of action would be to drive to town and send a cable to your family to ask if your sister has made contact. Should they have news, would your parents know where to wire it to you?"

"No." How stupid of her. Perhaps her father had already found Lizbeth and here she was, still searching and wasting other people's time. "You are right. I should do that."

Just then, a man on a bicycle appeared in the distance, pedalling fast on the dirt track.

"I think that's my foreman. Something must be wrong. Excuse me."

Arthur kicked his horse and galloped towards the man.

Shona and Will exchanged glances and rode after him.

Chapter 35

"**A** fire has broken in the workers' lines, Tuan!" The foreman was drenched in sweat.

Shona had been shown the workers' dwellings and had noticed that the homes were just sections of a long building. A fire would easily spread from one to the other.

Arthur frowned. "Is Tuan Reggie there?"

"We've tried to call him but we cannot find him."

Arthur turned to Will and Shona. "I'm sorry but I have to leave you."

"We're coming too." Shona glanced at Will who nodded.

When they got there, the fire was still spreading. Arthur and Will organised the fire-fighting efforts while Shona made sure the women and the children were safe and any injuries were tended.

It was a few hours before the fire was conquered and the workers could return to their homes—or what was left of some of them.

"Six families are without a home. Where can they spend the night?" Shona asked Arthur, fretting.

"My bungalow and Reggie's have spacious servants' quarters. Between the two of us we can accommodate them. What's more, if Reggie can't give me a good reason for being unreachable when I needed him, he can host all the six families in his own bed!"

Arthur and Shona left Will to assess the damage with the foremen and walked up to Reggie's bungalow. A couple of frangipane flowers lay on the steps to the house though Shona noticed there were no frangipane plants nearby. Laughter rang inside the bungalow, male and female, and the door was wide open.

Arthur was about to barge in but Shona touched his arm. "It may be unwise to go in unannounced."

Just then, a man and a girl in a white dress shot out of another door that led into the veranda, laughing and giggling like children playing chase.

"Lizbeth!"

Her sister stopped dead in her tracks and the man almost ran into her but caught himself in time. Then he saw Shona and Arthur and blanched.

"Shona!" Her sister smiled.

Her beautiful, beloved face was framed by a simple white veil and a crown of frangipane flowers.

Arthur turned to Shona. "I gather we've found your sister."

"Yes," Shona replied, shocked.

Lizbeth had married Arthur's assistant? But "Reggie" didn't start with "A".

Shona gathered her wits and let Arthur demand explanations first.

"Right, Reginald Adam Jones, explain yourself!" Arthur instructed sternly, sitting down on a wicker chair and steepling his fingers.

"I'm sorry, sir."

Reggie scratched the back of his head like a schoolboy caught red-handed.

He had sweet, brown eyes and looked to be as young as her sister.

"You don't even know what to be sorry about! What's been happening here, and why were you unavailable during a fire emergency?"

"A fire?" Reggie cried. "I'm awfully sorry, sir, I know nothing about any fire. I was in town—getting married! Are there casualties?"

"No, thanks to the foremen and my two new friends; one of whom, I believe, is your new sister-in-law."

Shona waved her fingers in a friendly greeting and smiled at the young man.

"Shall we have some drinks?" Lizbeth suggested practically.

They sat on the veranda and, drinks in hands, began to unravel the strange events.

"You know that you're not allowed to get

married until the end of your first contract, don't you?" Arthur scolded Reggie.

"Yes, sir, I do know that. The trouble was that Elizabeth was about to return to England and we didn't want to wait. I won't ask for the marriage allowance and this bungalow is plenty big enough for us. We will not ask them for anything. In fact, the company doesn't even need to know, does it?"

So this was the reason for the secrecy. Reggie's work contract didn't allow him to marry at this time.

Arthur ran a hand over his face. "That's all very well but what am I supposed to do? Pretend I don't know that there's a woman in the plantation?"

"Plenty of planters have women living with them secretly," Reggie pointed out.

Shona thought of Albert and his clandestine family.

"They are local women! Don't you think that a white woman will be noticed in the plantation? Out of it too." Arthur turned to Lizbeth. "You will want to shop in town, visit the club and play bridge with other women."

"No, I won't," she responded.

"Nonsense. You will go crazy after a few weeks of isolation up here."

"I have my husband and that's all I need for now."

Her sister's chin was set, her expression undaunted. Shona admired her. She knew that Lizbeth could do this. Despite her young age, she had more courage than herself.

Shona had crossed her father only by accident—first by being out of the home overnight and then by failing to restrain her tongue in a moment of high emotion. Her sister, in contrast, had stood up against their father, their society and the company's rules with cold premeditation. All her life Shona had waited for opportunities to be given her. Her sister had taken what hadn't been given her.

It was time for Shona to snatch her freedom too. She could do it. From now on she wasn't going to wait for anyone's permission. She would take charge of her own future.

Chapter 36

Reggie poured Arthur another stengah as they began discussing the practical arrangements for the new situation.

Shona took her sister aside. "Why didn't you tell me?"

"I didn't want to put you in a difficult situation. You'd have felt that you had to stop me," her sister explained. "I knew you would read my journal and find me."

"Reggie doesn't start with 'A', though!"

"I didn't think about that. I call him by his middle name—Adam."

"What was all that excitement about Danny and Bertie at the party?"

"Oh, did I mislead you? Sorry. They were our wedding witnesses and I wanted to discuss the arrangements for the wedding. They picked us up early this morning, drove us to town and signed the registry."

Shona's mind was reeling. Her sister had organised her own wedding without help from her family and in complete secret. "Do Maman and Papa know yet?"

"No."

"Papa is convinced you were abducted. He's searching for you, determined to bring your 'abductor' to justice. He's involved the police and the Forces."

Lizbeth looked horrified. "We must send a wire home at once!"

"Well, I suggest you keep your husband out of Papa's reach until you've explained everything to him."

They sent the houseboy with instructions for the wire.

Lizbeth turned to her. "Thank you for coming all the way here to warn me. I thought you'd read my journal, tell Maman and Papa and they'd believe you. I intended to write with more details once we were married."

"Why didn't you leave a note? Papa might have believed your words in a letter."

"I didn't want to make it too easy for him to find me, in case he stopped us." She took Shona's hands in hers. "I never imagined that you'd undertake such a journey. Tell me you weren't on your own."

Just then, Will appeared on the veranda.

"He accompanied me," Shona told her sister. "I didn't know any planters so I asked Will and he offered to come with me."

Lizbeth gave a mischievous smile. Shona hadn't wanted to admit she'd been with Will to avoid this sort of speculation. She had wronged him so much, though, that she had to give him credit for his invaluable, generous assistance. "I wouldn't be here without his help."

Shona had believed that men clipped women's wings, yet Will had done the opposite. He had given her wings and freedom to reach her sister before her father, to prevent a disastrous family rift.

She had fallen in love with him, then hated him. She admitted she had never stopped being in love with him.

Now that they'd found her sister, their ways would part forever. The thought of that broke her heart.

It could not be otherwise, though. She had rejected Will too many times to expect him to welcome her back.

Lizbeth invited her and Will to spend the night in their bungalow, quickly taking on the role of hostess. Shona didn't think it fair to impose company on the newlyweds on their wedding night, however.

"Don't be silly. We will be putting up three families here tonight. Would I turn out my sister?" Lizbeth said.

"They're staying in the servants' quarters, not in your guestrooms, Lizbeth."

Shona wasn't refusing only for her sister's sake. Staying there with Will, as if they were an actual couple, would make her feel more acutely the sadness of not being one.

"Thank you, but we mustn't. Arthur is expecting us at his bungalow," Will replied, ever the considerate gentleman.

"Then you must promise that you'll pop over and say goodbye to us before you and Will go back to Singapore, Shona," Lizbeth conceded.

"We are not going back together," Shona said, and turned to Will. "You have done for me so much more than I could have expected or deserved. I will make my own way back."

"Don't refuse a lift, sister," Lizbeth warned. "Transports are difficult up here, as Adam can confirm." She turned to her new husband who nodded. "Not only that, you could also miss the ship to England!"

Imagine that, missing the steamer…

Shona shook the thought away.

"I am heading back to Singapore anyway," Will pointed out.

"It would be unkind to deprive Will of company when you're both going in the same direction," her sister continued.

Shona was too tired to offer further resistance. "Thank you, Will. I accept the lift."

Chapter 37

Arthur had already done muster and despatched the workers by the time Will and Shona came down for breakfast.

Will had stayed in his room until he'd heard Arthur come back so that he wouldn't find himself alone with Shona. Since their argument on their first night at Arthur's, things had been awkward between them. Now their final goodbye was approaching, he was afraid he might let slip how much he was going to miss her and that he was still in love with her. That would be totally inappropriate, considering what she thought of him.

When they finally set off from Arthur's place, they headed towards Reggie's bungalow to fulfil their promise to Shona's sister.

The bungalow wasn't on their way and the detour made no sense logistically, but the two sisters weren't going to see each other for a long time. Lizbeth would remain in Malaya while Shona would be in England—or wherever else her wishes or her future husband would take her. Will didn't want even to think about the second possibility.

Shona looked sad as they rode towards the bungalow.

"Your sister will be fine. She seemed very happy with Reggie last night and he appears to be a thoroughly nice chap," he said, trying to cheer her up.

"Yes," she replied.

"If they have children soon, she'll have plenty to distract her, too."

"Yes."

"I saw many books on Reggie's shelves and Arthur has a gramophone," Will persisted. "She'll enjoy Arthur's company, I'm sure."

"I believe so."

"I will drop in on them every time I'm back in Johor. I'll send you news, if you wish it," he offered.

She turned to him. "'Back in Johor'? Where are you going?"

"I've decided to go to Borneo."

"Why?"

"There's more wilderness there." *And no memories of you.*

He wanted to ask her where she would be; what was her new address; could they keep in touch? He didn't, though. Shona had made it abundantly clear that she wanted him out of her life.

When they reached Reggie's bungalow, the car belonging to the District Officer was parked at the front. Hopefully this did not signal trouble for the young couple.

"Whose is this car?"

"I'm not sure."

Will didn't want to alarm Shona and he could be mistaken, after all.

They tied their ponies to the veranda's rail, climbed the steps and let themselves in through the open patio door.

In the living room were four people: Reggie and Elizabeth, looking tense and guarded; the D.O. … and Shona's father.

Shona let out a small gasp and the District Officer turned.

"Will Palmer, what a jolly surprise!" he said with a smile.

At that, Mr Wells turned. As he took in the sight of Will and Shona, his frown deepened.

"You two together again?" he barked, then recovered himself and smiled at the D.O. "This is my daughter, Shona. I gather you already know her fiancé."

The D.O.'s eyebrows lifted in surprise. He had often heard Will declare in the past that he wasn't marriage material.

"Well, double congratulations, then, Reginald!" he told Mr Wells, patting his back.

It all felt like déjà vu, harking back to that morning in Pulau Ubin when Mr Wells had arranged Shona's future with Will without consulting her. Will couldn't let it happen again, even if it meant contradicting, humiliating and making an enemy of a powerful man like Mr Wells.

He cleared his voice. "I'm afraid that's not the case. Shona has rejected my marriage proposal."

He saw shock on the faces of everyone present except for Mr Wells and Shona herself. So she had already told her father that she didn't want to marry him? Will's secret hope that she might change her mind crumbled away.

"Nonsense. Girls like to play hard to get," Mr Wells responded in a forced, playful tone.

The elopement of his other daughter proved him false, of course. He must have realised the absurdity of his statement because he reddened.

"When they go gallivanting about with young men, it's clear that they do wish to marry them," he argued, staring hard at Shona.

"Shona, only you can answer. Are you going to marry Will?" Lizbeth asked.

Shona's eyes were shiny.

Will longed to take her hand and squeeze it but he feared she wouldn't want him to touch her. He wished he was another man, one she was willing to marry, by whom she would let herself be comforted.

He wanted to tell her that she mustn't be troubled, that it was okay to reject him. He could take it. He had got the message.

He couldn't tell her all this in front of all these people. That was what Will regretted most about their sorry story. They had always ended up discussing marriage in front of others.

"Will is correct. I said no," she said in a quiet voice.

His lungs emptied completely. Even though he had expected this answer, his heart had hoped for a different one. There was no hope left.

"The only reason that Will and I are here together is that he has been very kind in helping me trace Lizbeth," Shona clarified and turned to him. "Thank you, Will. Now, if you don't mind, I will travel back with my father."

Chapter 38

O f course David and Catherine wanted to know all about his trip, but Will didn't feel like saying much. He was already missing Shona.

They had parted in public and had not exchanged correspondence addresses. He felt bereft.

He packed his trunks so that he could leave for Borneo first thing in the morning and, after a quick nightcap with his friends—carefully avoiding any talk of Shona—he said goodnight and turned in.

He fell asleep immediately and dreamt of her. The steamer taking her to England had sunk in the ocean and she was a castaway. He went to rescue her in his motorboat but she refused point blank to climb onboard.

Will woke up, sweaty and upset, to the sound of the koel bird singing its plaintive two notes.

He pushed away the mosquito net and looked out the window. Bats were still flying around the mango tree and the petals of the hibiscus and the jasmine remained wrapped for the night. From the top floor of the bungalow he could see the sea as far as Tanah Merah and Bedok.

He thought of Shona. She must be packed and ready to go, just like him. The difference was that she wasn't thinking of him while he couldn't stop thinking of her.

He ate a quiet breakfast on his own. When he was about to leave, David, Catherine and the children came down to say goodbye.

"Will you come back soon?" Jonah wanted to know.

"I will do my best, sir," Will replied, ruffling the little boy's hair.

Jonah's sister gave him a goodbye card she had painted and David hugged his friend.

"You'll miss your bus if you don't set off now, old sport," he told him, stepping back.

"He shouldn't be taking the bus with all this luggage," Catherine commented fretfully.

"I'm perfectly capable," Will replied, amused.

Catherine ignored him and turned to her husband. "You must drive him to his boat or call a taxi, David."

Will laughed. "Nonsense. I'm quite happy with taking the bus."

"He's just saying this so as not to put you to any trouble," Catherine reasoned with David.

"I can't take him, darling, I have to be in the office early today. What I could do is to send him with the driver and take a taxi myself," her husband proposed.

"I actually want to take the bus!" Will protested.

He was growing a trifle irritated but neither of his friends were paying attention to him.

It was ridiculous that David and Catherine should discuss his travel arrangements without giving him a say in the matter. Even more crazy that they had decided what his feelings about it must be.

Wait! Had he done the same with Shona? When she had told him that she wouldn't marry him, he had concluded that it was because she didn't love him.

After she had chosen to return to Singapore with her father and had said goodbye in public, without offering to keep in touch, he had concluded she must dislike him so much that they couldn't even be friends.

All this he had thought without consulting her just as Catherine had convinced herself that Will didn't want to take the bus.

Shona had never said she didn't love him. On the beach of the sailing club, when he had asked her father for her hand, she had told him she was never going to marry him. That wasn't the same thing.

She had told him to stay away from her but this, too, didn't mean she didn't love him. It meant that she was angry with him.

In Arthur's bungalow she had called him a cad,

a liar and a petulant child. Never had she told him that she hated him or didn't love him. People could be angry and yet be in love. He knew that very well.

A light of hope shone through the hole that Shona had left in his heart. She might never forgive him nor want to marry him but he needed to know if she had ever had feelings for him. If the answer was yes, then he could treasure the memories of their time together like a precious gift.

He dropped his luggage on the steps. "What time does the steamer for England leave?"

David and Catherine smiled at each other. "Seven-thirty."

That left little time.

"Take the car," David offered.

"A bicycle would go further through the crowds at the harbour," Catherine suggested.

It was odd how they both knew where he was going and why. Had Will been the only one not to see what needed to be done?

∞∞∞

He pedalled to the harbour as if his life depended on it—because it did. He would never forgive himself if he missed this last chance.

The streets around the harbour were already bustling. Even the sea was crowded with ocean liners and cargo steamers queueing outside the harbour walls for their turn to dock.

Will wove his way through people bidding farewell to family and friends. The P&O steamer blew its horn. Sailors were lifting the gangway. No!

He skidded to a halt at the end of the quay but the ship had already pushed out. He cupped his mouth with his hands and bellowed Shona's name. His voice echoed against the cobalt sky.

"Shona!" he called again.

Then he saw her. She was just a splash of colour on the deck but he recognised the flowery dress she had worn on the day of their trip to the mangroves.

"Shona!"

He waved his arms but she stayed motionless. Had she seen him? He would give anything to turn back time and reach here a few minutes earlier.

"Shona Wells!"

He watched dismally as the ship sailed away until it was nothing more than a dot on the horizon. He bent over, held his knees and breathed slowly. There was nothing he could do now.

Or maybe there was…

He mounted the bicycle and pedalled hard. If Shona was a member of the sailing club, they must have her forwarding address in the UK. Whether they would give it to him was another matter, but it was his best bet.

When he arrived at the club, he was drenched in sweat. The fronds of the traveller's palm waved in the breeze like a welcoming hand.

Will buttoned up his collar, smoothed his hair and summoned every ounce of charm and suavity he had.

"May I see the manager, please?"

Chapter 39

T hank goodness, this time they had given her a boat she could sail on her own. Shona tightened the boom vang and checked the tiller. Soon she'd be out on the sea, holding the wind in her hands.

This time the wind wasn't the only thing in her hands: her life and her future were there too.

In the end, it had been easier than she had expected. Her parents hadn't been pleased when she'd announced that she wasn't following them back to England, but they hadn't fought her. Maybe it was because they had accepted that she was now an old maid, or because her sister would be staying in Malaya.

It had taken Lizbeth eloping for Shona to take her future into her own hands and demand independence. Her father had relinquished control over her dowry with what had looked like relief. He must have tired of the impossible task of marrying her off.

However, on her first day in her new

independent life, she wasn't as happy as she had imagined. Because of Will.

She had loved him sincerely, passionately and wholeheartedly. She had also misunderstood, insulted and rejected him so many times that he couldn't ever forgive her.

She must stop thinking about him.

She slackened the mainsheet and reached for the rope that tethered the boat to the jetty, then froze. On the wooden boards was a familiar figure.

Her heart leaped into her throat as her gaze met Will's.

"Are you hiring crew for your trip?" he asked in his low, gravelly voice.

She tried to laugh. "After my last shipwreck, I'm unlikely to get any takers."

"That wasn't a shipwreck. It was enemy sabotage."

"I thought you regarded monkeys as friends, not foes."

"Anyone who upsets you is my foe."

"Then I'm your worst foe, and mine, too," she remarked lightly.

"We all are our worst foes."

He folded his long legs and sat down on the jetty, leaning on his palms. His golden legs dangled above the water in a charmingly boyish way.

He leaned forward. "What type of magical creature are you, who can be here now yet on a steamer headed for England half an hour ago?"

"You've been to the harbour?"

"Yes."

It didn't mean he had gone for her, though. He could have been there to bid farewell to other friends.

"I saw you on the ship," he went on.

"It must have been another woman."

"She was wearing the dress you wore the day we went to the mangrove."

He remembers my dress. "You must have seen my youngest sister. We look alike and I gave her the dress."

He nodded. "This still doesn't explain why you're not on that boat."

She wanted to ask him whether he wished she was, but she might not like the answer.

"I prefer sailing on boats that I can steer myself," she said finally.

He smiled and a little piece of the armour around her heart crumbled away.

"What brings you here, Will?"

He hadn't come to see her, he was just passing by, she told herself.

"I came to try to force the club manager to give me your address in England."

Hope edged its way into her heart. He had come because of her!

Why? She had insulted him. Twice she had told him she didn't want to marry him, and once she had shouted at him to stay away from her!

"Now I don't need to because I've found you." He smiled and his lovely dimples came out to play.

"Of course I won't force you to give me your address. You can sail away without giving me anything at all." He gestured to her hand which was resting loosely on the rope that tied her boat to the jetty.

"I will not stop you, either, because that choice is ultimately yours, Shona. It has always been and always will be. That was why I contradicted your father when he told the D.O. we were engaged."

"And because you had changed your mind about it," she challenged.

She couldn't accept he would still want to marry her.

He frowned. "Is that what you thought?"

"Yes."

"And is that why you said you wouldn't marry me?"

She thought she saw hope in his eyes. "No, I didn't do that."

"You didn't say it or didn't say it for that reason? Please explain, Shona. I'm desperate." He held his face in his hands.

"I only confirmed to my father that I had rejected you."

It was the only thing she could have said that was true. She couldn't have told him that she still loved him and had never stopped even when she had been furious at him. She couldn't have admitted that she was so terribly sorry for having misjudged him, insulted him and pushed him away. Most of all, she couldn't have confessed to him and everyone in the room that, now that he had stopped wanting her as his wife, she wanted to be.

"I shouldn't have asked your father for your hand in marriage before asking you, I know. Heaven knows I regret it. I do still love you, Shona. That hasn't changed, and probably never will, no matter what you do. That choice is mine. You can make me the happiest man in the world if you love me in return and agree to spend your life with me. That's your choice, though, and there's nothing I can do about it."

Her heart was suspended in the middle of her chest by strings of gossamer, beating frantically like skylark wings. She opened her mouth to speak but nothing came out.

"I know you don't love me back but, if you think there's a chance that one day you might, I will wait for as long as it takes—days, months, years. For me it's you or no one, Shona."

"I don't need time." She found her voice at last.

His chest dropped and he looked deflated. "I'm sorry. I shouldn't have cornered you like this."

He made to get up but she grabbed his wrist.

"I don't need time because I already know the answer. Will Palmer, I love you and I want to share my life with you!" Her voice broke.

He closed his eyes and let out a long breath.

"I'm not looking for crew for my boat," she added. "What I want is a co-captain."

A grin spread across his face and he slid down

into her boat, took her into his arms and kissed her. He tasted of sea, wild fruits and home.

"Where are we heading to?" he asked her.

She guessed he wasn't referring just to this morning's boat trip. "How about wherever there are plants to be discovered and nature to be protected?"

"You read my mind."

"Right now, though, I believe we should sail back to an island where a macaque mother and baby are waiting to hear our good news."

The End

Books By This Author

How To Choose A Husband

Grazia Colonna has waited fifty years to meet The One. Now that her best friend is getting married for the second time, Grazia is sure that she'll meet The One at Rebecca's wedding. He will sweep Grazia off her feet and snatch her from the clutches of her bullying mother.

But first Grazia needs to alter the dress she will wear at the event and, for this, she needs the help of the village's grumpy widower tailor, Hector Gonzales.

As the bride is stuck abroad and may not get back in time for the wedding, Grazia and Hector are forced to work together and, inconveniently, they fall in love.

Can they ensure that the right wedding goes ahead and the wrong one doesn't?

Sweet Competition For Camillo's Café

Camillo runs a popular café on Altavicia's main square. Giada runs an equally popular café across the square. They have both entered Altavicia's Best Café competition. Scarred by his father's death, Camillo's greatest wish is to escape the Calabrian seaside village and return to his beloved London, where his family was last together and happy. Abandoned by her parents, Giada's greatest wish is to earn her nonna's love. The competition trophy is the ticket to both their dreams, but only one can win. As Camillo discovers that happiness doesn't come from a location and Giada that love isn't earned, can enemies become friends, and maybe more?

Second Chances At Mamma's Trattoria

She's raised his daughters in secret at his mama's trattoria.

When Eleonora got a job at Mamma Cristina's trattoria, she didn't tell the sweet old woman that she was her son's ex-wife, nor that the twins are her granddaughters. Her plan was to give the twins a taste of family life without any of the trouble. But she had not planned for Davide to come home.

Davide loves his job at sea and he wouldn't have come home if it hadn't been for Mamma Cristina's health scare. The last thing he expected to find was his ex-wife implanted in the heart of his home with two young daughters in tow.

The last thing Eleonora and Davide want is to work together. But a celebrity Christmas wedding at the

trattoria requires every hand on deck.
How long can Eleonora and Davide avoid each other while working together and living under the same roof?

A secret-babies, enemies-to-lovers, second-chance romance set in Italy at Christmas.

The Italian Fake Date

When Alice Baker discovers that she's been adopted, she knows she won't have peace until she's found her Italian birth mother. But all she has is a letter written twenty-five years ago and an old address. Jaded about love and unable to forgive his ex-fiancée and his brother, Paolo Rondino is struggling to find inspiration for a sculpture that will make or break his career. Hoping that a trip home will help him find his muse again, he decides to return to Italy, even if this means confronting the two people who betrayed him. Alice and Paolo strike a deal: he will help her find her birth mother and she will pretend to be his girlfriend to please his mother. It looks like the perfect exchange, until real feelings start to grow...

Stars Are Silver

Is it too late for Melina to learn to drive? Is Don Pericle's vow never to fall in love again still valid after fifty years? Will a falling piano squash

Filomena or just shake up her heart? Why does the mother of the bride ask Don Pericle to cancel the wedding?

Tales From The Parish

Father Okoli dreams of owning a flock of hens and studying for a PhD, when his bishop saddles him with yet another parish to look after.

But as Father moves to Moreton-on-the-Edge, a farming village in the English Cotswolds, he's plugged into a community of warm-hearted characters, from the motherly parish secretary to her septuagenarian neighbour who's become a cycling champion, and from teenagers requiring driving lessons to atheist publicans who believe in miracles.

As the community pulls together to reopen the village's Electric Picture House, dreams are fulfilled, teen love blossoms and Father Okoli feels that Moreton-on-the-Edge is now home.

Drive Me Crazy

"Cohabitation is tribulation" goes an Italian saying, and after more than fifty years of married life, Tanino and Melina know a thing or two about the challenges of living together.

A Slip Of The Tongue

Will Melina regret faking to be sick to avoid her chores? Can Don Pericle organise a wedding for a groom who doesn't know? Who has stolen the marble pisces from the cathedral's floor?

What's Yours Is Mine

Can Melina give away her husband's possessions because they've always said that 'what's mine is yours and what's yours is mine'? Will the 'Sleep Doctor' deliver on his promises? How will the young Sicilian duke, Pericle, help his friend get married?

Fresh From The Sea

Will Gnà Peppina give her customers what they need, even if it's more than food? What pleasures can a man indulge in after his wife has put him on a draconian diet? Who will be able to cook dinner for the family with five euros?

Confetti And Lemon Blossom

For Don Pericle, wedding organising is a calling, not just a career. Deep in the Sicilian countryside, between rose gardens and trellised balconies, up marble staircases and across damasked ballrooms, these charming stories unfold.

A Season Of Goodwill

How far should Viviana's family go to avoid being thirteen at the table? Should Melina and Tanino attend a New Year's party hosted by Melina's old flame? Why do Don Pericle's clients want a Christmas wedding at all costs?

Sand, Sea & Tamburello

When Rosetta dries her hair on her balcony, she's not interested in the sun's warmth but in the young fishmonger who's eager to warm her heart. Can Don Pericle be a gracious host when an entire wedding party gets stranded at his villa? Tanino and Melina have a tough job competing with Valentina's other grandparents who take her on exhilarating trips to the beach. What can Alfonso do when his neighbours' karaoke parties become too much?

Father Roberto And The Missing Money

Two short cosy mysteries featuring a young Catholic priest in a Sicilian parish—perfect for fans of Father Brown, the Grantchester mysteries and the Mitford series.

The Holiday Heist:

When young Sicilian Catholic priest Father Roberto finds an envelope full of cash lying on the floor by the church's nativity scene, he assumes it's a Christmas donation for his cash-strapped parish. But it turns out that the unexpected windfall isn't for keeping, and it lands the inexperienced priest in a heap of trouble just at the parish's busiest time of year—the run-up to Christmas. Only by finding the real culprits can Father Roberto rid himself of the suspicion of robbery and get back to doing the job he loves.

The Missing Money:

In the seminary, nobody taught Father Roberto how to take a large group of children safely across a busy Palermo road. But as the young priest learns the ropes of being a children's summer camp leader for the parish, an unexpected problem emerges: the money put aside for the children's activities keeps disappearing.

Just as Roberto believes he's found the culprit, he discovers that the innocent are guilty and the guilty are innocent.

Father Roberto And The Runaway Ring

The Runaway Ring

When well-to-do parishioner, Signora Albi, asks Father Roberto to recommend a trustworthy housekeeper, he puts forward Tano. The teenage boy knows how to keep house and he badly needs a job to keep himself out of trouble.

But when Signora Albi's precious engagement ring goes missing, she has no doubt that Tano is the culprit and that the young priest is his unwitting accomplice.

Now Roberto must find the missing ring before Signora Albi's deadline if he is to get himself and his young friend off the hook.

The Elopers' Escapade

There's nothing Father Roberto likes more than praying in the empty church at night, when nobody can interrupt him. But an eloping couple has other ideas. Seeking refuge from their rival criminal families, the star-crossed lovers demand that Roberto marries them then and there. Roberto would normally turn to his superior, Father Pietro, but he's mysteriously missing.

Can Roberto find Father Pietro and keep the Sicilian Romeo and Juliet safe from their families?

Two heartwarming cosy mysteries featuring a young priest in a Sicilian parish—perfect for fans of Chesterton's Father Brown, Jan Karon's Mitford series and the Grantchester mysteries

Keeping It Cool

Every good mum knows how to keep her daughter safe. But how will Izzy's mum cope on a visit to a perilous ice rink? Josh thinks Elise's boyfriend wish list is rather unusual. Can he tick all the boxes? Mario knows that his name is as common in Italy as John Smith. But why are his friends sending him funeral wreaths? Ten humorous and uplifting stories, perfect for your coffee break.

Welcome To Quayside

Forty-year-old Tanya Baker dreams of starting a new life and making friends when she moves to a block of flats by the River Thames with her thirteen-year-old daughter, Hattie. But as Tanya and Hattie knock on neighbours' door in search of a tin opener, it's clear that the residents of Number One Quayside like to keep to themselves. Everyone, that is, except their next-door neighbours, Italian chef Giacomo Dalamo, and his thirteen-year-old daughter, Frankie. Between a delicious dish of lasagne (Giacomo's) and a burnt salad (Tanya's), they hatch a plan to set a library of things in their building, so that residents can borrow rarely-used items, from DIY tools to sports equipment and party supplies. First, though, Tanya and Giacomo must win over their neighbours, persuade the building's management company, source library stock by kayaking down the Thames, and deal with plumbing disasters, all the while trying to protect their bruised hearts from falling for each other.

Father Roberto And The Rural Riots

Two heartwarming cosy mysteries featuring a

young priest in a Sicilian parish—perfect for fans of Chesterton's Father Brown, Jan Karon's Mitford series and the Grantchester mysteries.

To Be Loved

Amanda's name means "to be loved" and she's taken it as her duty to make herself lovable, but it's hard work.

Has Tanino really abandoned Melina at home to freeze?

Mark hasn't seen Nora for thirty years and, since then, he's lost a leg and all his hair. If he wasn't enough for her then, can he be now?

What happens if the dating app's algorithms go haywire?

Good Habits

Sister Luce loves her quiet life in the convent in the Italian Apennine mountains. In the company of her hens, among chestnut groves and fir forests, the shy young nun is at her happiest.

But Mother Speranza has invited a TV crew into their convent to shoot a documentary about their life, and she asks Sister Luce to be the convent's poster girl.

Never has Sister Luce's vow of obedience been so sorely tested, especially when four worldly women come to share the convent's life under the camera's lens.

Between a Santa dash and a carnival float, a forest sit-in and a song competition, Sister Luce becomes performer, protester, agony aunt and equestrian nun as she learns to conquer her fears.

Divided into thirty-one short self-contained small chapters, this popular series from The People's Friend magazine includes one brand-new story never published before.

About The Author

Stefania Hartley

Stefania was born in Sicily but left her sunny island after falling in love with an Englishman. With her husband and their three children, she has lived in the Far East for many years. Now she's back in the UK.

She'd love you to leave a review where you bought this book and to sign up for her newsletter at: www.stefaniahartley.com/subscribe
so she can let you know when a new book is out. You'll also receive an exclusive short story.

www.ingramcontent.com/pod-product-compliance
Lightning Source LLC
Chambersburg PA
CBHW060437180626
46817CB00007B/2855